sew zoey

READY TO WEAR

written by
Chloe Taylor

illustrated by
Nancy Zhang

Simon Spotlight
New York   London   Toronto   Sydney   New Delhi

SIMON SPOTLIGHT
An imprint of Simon & Schuster Children's Publishing Division
1230 Avenue of the Americas, New York, New York 10020
Copyright © 2013 by Simon & Schuster, Inc.
All rights reserved, including the right of reproduction in whole
or in part in any form.
SIMON SPOTLIGHT and colophon are registered trademarks of
Simon & Schuster, Inc.
Text by Lara Bergen
Designed by Laura Roode
For information about special discounts for bulk purchases, please contact
Simon & Schuster Special Sales at 1-866-506-1949 or
business@simonandschuster.com.
Manufactured in the United States of America 0413 FFG
First Edition 10 9 8 7 6 5 4 3 2 1
ISBN 978-1-4424-7933-3 (pbk)
ISBN 978-1-4424-7934-0 (hc)
ISBN 978-1-4424-7935-7 (eBook)
Library of Congress Catalog Card Number 2013935204

CHAPTER 1

Creeeak...

Thud!

Zoey Webber heard the glamorous thump of glossy paper meeting floorboards, and raced down the hall to the front door to get the mail. Only one thing could make that sound: the newest issue of

Très Chic arriving through the mail slot.

Yes!

She scooped it up along with some envelopes and interior design magazines and put everything but *Très Chic* on a table for her aunt. Then she scanned the cover to see what was *très chic* for July:

The Long (Dresses) and Short (Shorts) of Summer Style

Dots Are Hot!

25 Fresh Fashion Faces to Watch

Be Inspired . . . by BOLD Colors!

Zoey grinned at the last headline. Oh, she *was* inspired.

She was also lucky. She was spending her summer days at Aunt Lulu's house instead of the usual: being stuck at home with her big brother, Marcus, as her babysitter, or stuck at day camp for what felt like the hundredth year in a row. This summer was different. Her brother was busy with a part-time job and her dad finally agreed that she was getting a little old for day camp . . . at least if she didn't want to go.

Zoey discovered pretty quickly that "Aunt Lulu camp" was better than any day camp. Aunt Lulu ran her interior design business out of her home office, but even when she had to work, she made it fun for Zoey. She let Zoey suggest fabrics and color combinations for clients' inspiration boards and make collages and paper doll clothes with old wallpaper samples. And if she had to go out for a meeting or something, she actually *paid* Zoey to dog-sit—which basically meant watching Aunt Lulu's fourteen-year-old mutt, Draper, snore.

Plus, Zoey and her aunt loved doing a lot of the same things: getting mani-pedis, baking cookies, reading magazines, watching old movies, and indulging in reality TV shows—they both were hands-down obsessed with fashion design competitions. Too bad Dad and Marcus couldn't stand them. "Boys will be boys," Aunt Lulu always said.

Zoey walked over to the kitchen table without taking her eyes off the magazine cover for a second. She sat down on a chair and then gently let the magazine's uncracked spine fall open to a random page. It landed on a perfume sample. It was the newest in a popular line of scents by a young fashion designer. Zoey closed her eyes and took a whiff, inhaling the amber and tuberose, and letting her mind wander. . . .

What if I were a fashion designer someday? she imagined. *I'd get to look at pretty clothes and read magazines all day long! Maybe I'd make my own perfume too, and it would smell like . . . um . . . gardenias? Yeah. And maybe one day I'd be in* Très Chic's "Day in the Life of a Designer" *section! How cool would that be if it really happened?*

It might have just been a daydream, but it sounded pretty amazing to Zoey. She sighed, put the magazine down on the table, and began to flip through the pages, scanning each spread to make sure she saw every square inch of it.

Beep-beep.

Zoey quickly lifted her head. Did she hear a beeping sound?

Yep, that was definitely her phone saying a text had just come in!

"Coming!" she yelled toward the muffled ringtone. She stood up and looked around the kitchen.

Beep-beep.

She twirled in place. Where exactly *was* her phone? She was sure she'd left it on the table . . . but it wasn't there.

Maybe on the kitchen counter? Nope. She even checked inside the fridge.

She crawled around under the table in case it had dropped on the floor. Still no luck!

"Excuse me, Draper," she said as she gently slid her hand under his belly. Maybe he fell asleep on top of her phone? His ear twitched and his leg kicked, but his snoring never stopped. She groaned and started to get up.

Beep-beep.

Okay . . . her phone had to be somewhere . . . somewhere very close. She had spent most of the morning planted at the kitchen table drawing imaginary outfits in her newest sketchbook. It was her favorite thing to do at Camp Lulu by far.

At the beginning of summer, Aunt Lulu noticed all the fashion drawings Zoey was doing on the back of used printer paper and started hanging them on the fridge.

When there was no space left in the "art gallery," as Aunt Lulu started to call it, she surprised Zoey with a beautiful sketchbook tied with a big raffia bow. "I'm glad you're saving the Earth, but drawings like yours deserve to be on something better than scrap paper, don't you think?" she had asked. "Plus, I don't want you to lose any of them!"

And the rest, as they say, was history—soon Zoey had filled a few sketchbooks with original clothing designs. Well, some were inspired by her favorite designers, like Blake and Bauer and the amazing Daphne Shaw, especially in the beginning. But most of them were unique, and her aunt loved them all. She loved the silly ones, like the "sunny day sundress" made of sky-blue fabric dotted with puffy white clouds. And she even loved the unwearable ones, like the flapper dress made entirely of those plastic rings that hold together six-packs of soda cans. Zoey didn't show the sketchbooks to anyone else. Not even to her best friends, Priti and Kate. She just did it for fun . . . and because once she got started, she couldn't stop coming up with ideas.

It was pretty funny, actually, that she spent so

much time dreaming up different outfits. During the school year, she had to wear the same exact thing every single day: five days a week of a standard-issue school uniform. Sometimes she wondered if she would be so obsessed with clothes if she actually got to wear them!

But right now she had a much more vital question on her mind: Where on earth was her phone?

Wait . . . her sketchbook was looking awfully thick.

She flipped through the pages . . . and *there* it was! On top of a drawing of a floor-skimming maxi dress and a scallop-edged white tank paired with geometric-print pedal pushers.

She laughed, breathed a sigh of relief, and looked down at the screen to see who was sending all those texts.

Can you believe it?! said the first text. Then there was a: **Hello??** Finally came an: **Um, Zoey? R u there?**

The text messages were from Priti Holbrooke, one of Zoey's two very best friends.

Zoey picked up her phone and gawked at the screen as a million thoughts flew through her head.

Believe *what*? She had no idea!

And was it good? (She hoped!)

Or bad . . . (Uh-oh!)

Priti! Zoey loved her because she knew how to make life more exciting. But sometimes she could give you a heart attack!

Zoey thumbed back a speedy, desperate reply: **Believe what?!?!**

She clutched her phone and waited, staring at the screen. . . .

Still, she jumped when it beeped and blinked to life again.

No more uniforms! texted Priti.

Zoey's mouth fell open and she nearly dropped the phone. "No way!" she cried out loud, reading it over again to be sure.

Could it be that after sixty-five years, Mapleton Prep was finally waking up? Could it be that the petition Zoey started last spring had actually worked? She started it because she didn't feel like everyone else, and she didn't want to *dress* like everyone else, either. But she never thought it would work.

The school wasn't really that bad overall. The

classrooms had big windows. Most of the teachers were nice. And except for the gelatinous meat loaf and cardboard pizza, the food was mostly edible. It was just those uniforms! All that horrible gray polyester. And those plaid ties. Every time Zoey got dressed for school in them, she could swear a part of her soul died.

R u sure? she texted back.

Yes! +!!!!!!!! came the answer right away.

Zoey did a little dance of joy and quickly pressed call instead of reply.

"Hi!" answered Priti.

"How did you find out? Are you sure?" Zoey blurted.

"Zoey, we got a letter in the mail!" Priti told her. "Haven't you seen it? It came today!"

Zoey groaned. "Ugh, I missed it! I'm at my aunt's house. What does it say?"

"Hang on." Zoey could hear Priti moving around and shuffling some papers. "It's here some-where . . . *Tara!*" Priti hollered to one of her sisters as Zoey pulled the phone away from her ear. "Where's the mail? I need that letter from my school!"

While she waited, Zoey could picture the likely scene taking place in the Holbrooke home. There was always a lot going on with three girls as lively as Priti and the twins. Tara and Sashi were in high school, and each had their own *niche*, as their dad liked to say. Sashi played the piano . . . and the flute and the harp, and sang, too. Her primary goal in life these days was earning a scholarship to Juilliard. Tara, on the other hand, was all about biology and organic chemistry and basically anything that screamed pre-med. She was spending the summer working in a college lab.

Priti was the baby of the family and the opposite of her focused, organized older sisters. Her grades were fine and her work was never late. And yet her bedroom and her backpack might as well have been black holes. She wasn't exactly a slob . . . but maybe she was, a little bit. Whatever she lacked in organizational skills, however, she more than made up for in overall spunk and charm. Zoey could always count on Priti to cheer her up if she was feeling down. Or to make her laugh until her stomach hurt.

"Sorry about that, Zoey," Priti said. "Zoey? Are you still there?"

"Yes!" Zoey answered. "Read it to me! Hurry! Who's the letter from?"

"Our new principal," Priti told her. "Her name is Ms. Austen. Ms. *Esther* Austen . . . Esther? What a name, right? Anyway, 'Dear Students and Families,' she says, 'I hope this letter finds you well and that you are enjoying your summer' . . . blah, blah, blah, you get the idea."

"*Yes!*" Zoey said, tapping her fingers on the table.

"Okay . . . 'As well as introducing myself, I'm writing to announce some exciting changes at Mapleton Preparatory. First, we will be expanding the music department—'"

"*Music department!*" Zoey groaned. "Priti. You're killing me. Get to the uniform part, please!"

"Patience, patience," Priti teased her. "Just kidding. Here it is . . . 'And finally, after extensive thought and debate, we will no longer be requiring students to wear uniforms.'" She paused and waited for Zoey's reaction. "Zoey? Are you there? Did you faint or something?"

Zoey, meanwhile, had sunk like a rock into the kitchen chair. She still had the phone to her ear, but her mind had zoomed a million miles away. She immediately had visions of Mapleton's hallowed halls full of kids—dressed in *colors* and *patterns* and *natural fabrics* instead of industrial-strength polyester—being allowed to look like individuals for once!

"Zoey?"

"I'm here! I just can't believe it! Does it say anything else?"

"Yeah, I mean I guess there'll still be a kind of 'dress code,' and it goes on about that . . . no short skirts, no tube tops, that kind of thing. No big logos . . . Oh well. It's a start. But you can read all that stuff at home. Right now we need to decide when we're going to go shopping and where! You know how my mom always makes me wear my sisters' hand-me-downs? Well, listen to this! She said that I can actually go shopping for first-day-of-school clothes this year! So we have to do it right away, before she changes her mind."

"Then let's go this weekend!" Zoey said quickly.

"Yay!" said Priti. "To the mall?"

"Sure," Zoey said. "And hey, have you talked to Kate yet? Oh gosh!" She suddenly had another thought. "What's her mom going to do?"

Kate's mom was, hands down, one of the nicest moms in the whole world. In fact, she'd been like a second mom to Zoey ever since her own mom passed away. Zoey had only been two when it happened, so she didn't remember her mother so well. It helped to think her mom was something like Mrs. Mackey.

Mrs. Mackey did something called "strategic planning" for the university, which Zoey gathered meant looking ahead and which always seemed a little ironic to her since Kate's mom's style was so . . . stuck in the past. And, of course, maybe she liked it that way. If there was any rule to fashion, thought Zoey, it was that it's a totally personal thing. The only problem was Mrs. Mackey's style had a serious impact on Kate. Like the dress she got Kate for the softball banquet last spring. It looked like it was meant for a six-year-old: It was made of gingham and had a sash *and* a Peter Pan collar and these enormous puffy sleeves. Honestly, Kate was the one person for whom school uniforms had been a *good* thing. Turning her mom loose on any other school wardrobe would be a very dangerous thing.

"We have to run interference," said Zoey.

"Of course!" Priti agreed. "I'll text her right now and see if she's read the letter, and I'll tell her we're taking her shopping ASAP!"

"*Yippee!* I can't wait!" said Zoey, jumping back up. She couldn't contain her excitement anymore and let out a joyful squeal.

"Zoey! Is everything okay?"

Zoey turned to see her aunt Lulu running in from the laundry room with a basket of freshly dried clothes. Her normally relaxed face wore a look of worried surprise.

"What's wrong?" Aunt Lulu gasped. "I heard you scream from the laundry room!"

"Nothing! Sorry!" Zoey said with a smile. "Everything's amazingly, awesomely fine! Gotta go, Priti. Call me as soon as you talk to Kate," she told Priti, hanging up. "Guess what, Aunt Lulu! My school's getting rid of uniforms!"

Her aunt looked relieved. "Phew! Well, it's about time. It's just middle school, not the army!"

"I know, right?" Zoey said. She held out her arms to grab the laundry basket. "Here, can I help you with that . . . Uh-oh, what happened?" she said, looking down.

There was something about the laundry that didn't quite look right. . . . The clothes were the same exact shade of Pepto-Bismol pink.

Aunt Lulu sighed and reached into the pocket of a newly pink shirt and pulled out a piece of red velvet the size of a handkerchief. "Um, if you could remind me not to put red fabric samples in my white shirt pockets again, I'd really appreciate it," she said.

"Oh, Aunt Lulu!" Zoey winced . . . and swallowed a laugh at the same time. "Well, look on the bright side," she said. "You look *great* in bright pink!"

CHAPTER 2

"What do you think?" Priti held up a tiered miniskirt that resembled a fiery sunset.

Kate looked over and knitted her eyebrows. "I thought we couldn't wear miniskirts," she said.

"Oh yeah." Priti frowned. "But it's so *cute*! I love it!" she went on.

"Well, you could always put it over leggings," said Zoey, flipping through another rack. "Or this one?" Zoey held up a gauzy shirt in a teal blue that looked great next to Priti's skin. "It's so *you*. Bright and cheery. What do you think? It would work with those red jeans we saw earlier and maybe a skinny white belt? Last month's *Très Chic* has a whole feature about color blocking!"

"Sold!" Priti said, crossing over and snagging the shirt from Zoey's hand. "Ooh, and how about this?" She nodded to a floral, flutter-sleeved shirt on the very same rack. It had two layers of ruffles at the neck and sequins all along the hem.

"Whoa! That's a lot of sparkle," said Zoey.

"Too much?" Priti cocked her head.

"Well . . ." Zoey twisted her mouth and thought for a second. "For me . . . yes. Definitely too much of a good *bling*. But if you like it, go for it." She smiled and shrugged.

Priti grinned and with a dramatic swoop, added the top to the pile on her arm. "Good! I'm buying it. Well, unless it's hideous when I try it on."

Zoey nodded and turned from Priti to Kate,

whose tan arms were still empty. She was twirling her long ponytail around her finger. Her hair was still damp from her early swim meet, and she had on her bathing suit under her shorts and her favorite Mapleton Soccer tee.

"Kate. What's up? You don't have anything to try on."

"Ugh. I know." Kate sighed. "But everything's so 'Here I am. Look at me,' you know? Can't I just leave it at jeans and a T-shirt and call it done?"

"No, you cannot!" Zoey crossed her arms and made a mock-offended face. "Jeans and a T-shirt? You're totally missing the point," she said.

"There's a point?" asked Kate, smiling. She wasn't usually sarcastic, but Zoey was practically a sister. They'd known each other forever.

"The point," said Zoey, "is that we finally have the chance to wear whatever we want. After all these years of dressing alike, we can finally be ourselves and stand out from the crowd."

"But . . ." Kate shrugged and tucked her hands into her elbows. "I don't want to stand out," she said. She gazed along her lean legs to the flip-flops on her long, slender feet. "You know me, Zoey. I *like* blending in."

Zoey sighed. It was true. That was how Kate had always been. It was still a joke, for instance, how way back in kindergarten she hated playing tag. It made her feel like she had a big target on her back. She probably would have had more fun if she was ever tagged "it" and got to be the one doing the chasing . . . but she was too fast to get caught. She even outran the boys.

Her mom took that as a sign that she was a natural athlete and enrolled her in every sport imaginable. And everything changed. Kate became a different person on the field. She could just focus on the ball and forget everyone and everything around her. Zoey could hardly remember how shy Kate was before she found sports. But Kate could still be self-conscious sometimes. Especially about things that were outside her comfort zone. And this was one of those times.

If it was up to Kate, there would be a uniform for school and for everywhere else too. Kate loved her swim-team swimsuit, her softball uniform, and her soccer jersey. But she had signed Zoey's no-more-uniforms petition last year—and even helped pass it around—because Zoey was her oldest, dearest friend. Kate was great like that, even though she would have preferred to not change a thing. So Zoey bit her tongue. How could she give Kate a hard time for wanting to keep her first-day-of-school outfit simple?

"And besides," Kate went on with a teasing smirk, "what do you have so far, Miss Fashion Guru?"

Zoey looked down guiltily at the lone tank top she was holding. "I know. What can I say? I'm not having much luck, either." She looked back up at her friends and then let her eyes roam the racks of clothes. "I think my problem is that I have something in mind," she said. "And I don't think I see it here."

"What do you mean?" asked Priti.

"I have an idea of what I want to wear . . . but I'm starting to wonder if it even exists."

"Well, let us help you find it!" Priti said.

"Should we look somewhere else?" Kate asked.

"There are a lot more stores in the mall. Though . . . maybe we should eat first. . . . I'm starving. Food. That's what I want. Are there any good stores on the way to the food court?"

"Kate, it's only eleven thirty!" Priti laughed.

"Here. Want some gum?" Zoey reached in her bag and pulled out a pack.

Kate shook her head. "I shouldn't . . . the braces." Then she reached out her hand and took a piece. "Oh, what do I care? They're coming off soon. Thanks," she said, popping it into her mouth. "But remind me to spit it out before we meet my mom. She doesn't want me to chew gum and risk popping off another bracket."

"So what *are* you looking for, Zo?" asked Priti, whose braces weren't coming off soon, so she watched Zoey put the gum back into her bag.

Zoey shrugged. "I'd show you guys if I had my sketchbook," she said. "I've been drawing a bunch of ideas for clothes at Camp Lulu. Hey, do you want to come home with me and see them? Maybe you could sleep over?"

"I'm in!" said Priti instantly.

"Me too," said Kate. "Let's go ask my mom."

Mrs. Mackey had driven them all over after Kate's morning swim meet and had left them to shop on their own while she got her glasses fixed. She had the kind of lenses that turned into sunglasses as soon as she stepped outside. Somehow, though, one eye had stopped changing and was permanently dark.

"Hang on, guys!" Priti held up her free hand. "I still have to try all this stuff on!"

"Well, hurry," Kate said. "I could eat a shark."

Priti did her best to power through trying on the pieces she'd picked out, but she still had to decide what to buy.

"I think the key is getting a few basics," advised Zoey. "Things that mix and match with one another. And that you can totally reinvent depending on how you wear them. Like that hot pink cardigan with the funky buttons . . . You can wear it over a tank top," she told Priti, "*or* turn it around and button it up the back and push up the sleeves. It's like two for one!"

"Sold!" said Priti. "And I need the teal and floral shirts. And those black skinny jeans. And that adorable green skirt with the teensy-weensy polka dots." She paused for a second, holding up a pair of bright red jeans. "These are perfect, right?"

"Right," said Zoey. "They're so fun!"

"Okay, that's all true," added Kate. "But, Priti, that's a lot of clothes. Are you sure your parents are going to be okay with it?"

"Well, my mom took pity on me. It's my first time shopping for school, so she's letting me buy a few outfits," she said, but decided to keep the receipts, just in case.

Zoey stepped up to the register with a new pair of jeans, a navy-and-fluorescent-green-striped tank top with gold buttons on the side, and an *amazing* patterned bangle bracelet. Zoey slipped the bracelet on her wrist.

"I know this is going to sound funny, but this zigzag bracelet makes me happy," she said, smiling at Kate and Priti. "It'll go with everything, too."

"Awesome!" Priti said. "That's what my sisters call a 'signature accessory.' What about you, Kate? Did you find anything you love?"

Kate was clutching a few pairs of jeans and some T-shirts, but didn't look convinced. "I'm sorry, guys, but I really don't want these jeans, even if you like the way they look. I can't move in them," she said with a groan. Until, that is, Zoey reminded her of one important fact:

"You know, if you don't get *anything* new, Kate, you're going to have to wear your old *uniform* to school."

"Yeah, talk about standing out," Priti playfully informed her.

"Okay, fine." Kate sighed, letting a smile sneak out. She picked up a gray T-shirt and some jeans that were clearly a size too big for her.

"Are you sure about those?" asked Zoey.

"I'll grow into them," Kate said.

"Okay, but try this too," Zoey said, adding a preppy shirtdress to the pile. It was in Kate's favorite color, pale blue, and had a sporty white stripe down the side. It looked cute but comfy.

Mrs. Mackey walked in and found them just as Kate was getting ready to pay. Kate's mom was wearing her typical summer weekend ensemble—

a white shirt with the collar turned up and a pair of khaki pants embroidered with little green ducks. Her lenses had been fixed, and both eyes smiled eagerly at them.

"So, how did you girls do? Need any fashion advice?" she asked.

Zoey wisely rejected the temptation to look at Priti or Kate.

"Nope, we're all good, Mom. Zoey was like our own personal fashion consultant," Kate said. "But how about we stop for ice cream? I'm starving!"

"Sure!" said her mom. Then her grin turned to a frown. "Katherine Quinn Mackey! Are you chewing gum?"

CHAPTER 3

"Honestly, Zoey, these are just awesome!" Priti slowly turned through the pages of Zoey's latest sketchbook, pausing to ooh and aah over every one. "How'd you keep this a secret all summer? You're brilliant!"

"No, I'm not, I swear!" Zoey said shyly. "Anyway,

I didn't mean to keep it a secret. I just was doing them for fun . . . not to show anyone."

"Well, they're so cool!" Kate said, nodding as she leafed through the other older sketchbook. "Ooh! I like this dress—with the bows on the shoulders." She pointed to a red gown with a neckline that plunged into a deep V that Zoey had dreamed up after watching an awards show on TV.

"You do?" Zoey eyed her.

Priti peered over and looked surprised too.

Kate started to blush. "Not for *me*," she said quickly. "For someone, you know, grown up."

The girls were holed up in Zoey's bedroom, lined up like piano keys across her bed.

"Here's a dress I thought might work for school, if I could find it," Zoey told them, pointing at a sketch of a delicately pleated dress. "But I don't know if I love it anymore."

"I don't know what you're talking about," said Priti. "It's amazing! I knew you were a good artist, Zoey—but you're a born designer, too."

"A born designer? I wish!" Zoey said. Priti was probably exaggerating—as she sometimes did—

but the thought of it made Zoey's cheeks burn.

"Where do you get all these ideas?" Kate asked.

Zoey shrugged. "I don't know . . . Magazines? And TV, I guess. But mostly I just start drawing and somehow they just kind of . . . come out."

"You know what I think?" said Priti, suddenly serious.

Zoey looked at her. "No. What?"

"I think these would make for a really awesome blog."

Zoey's right eyebrow went up and she chuckled as she pushed herself to her knees. "Yeah. A blog. *Right*. So what do you guys want to do now?" she went on, dismissing the thought. "Want to see if my brother left any ice cream in the house?"

"Yes!" Kate started to spring up, but Priti pulled her back.

"I'm serious!" said Priti. "Can't you see it, Zoey?" She held up Zoey's open sketchbook in front of her and waited for her to nod.

But Zoey couldn't see it. Not at all. "What do you mean?" she asked.

"I mean a *blog*," said Priti. "Like the one Justin

Bieber has. Only about *this*." She pointed to Zoey's sketchbook. "Instead of about going on tour and stopping by the *TODAY Show* and being gorgeous."

Zoey laughed, then frowned. "Oh, come *on*. Who would read it?"

Priti shrugged. "I don't know."

"I do." Kate spoke up.

"Who?" asked Zoey.

"Us!"

"Ha-ha, thanks, Kate," Zoey said, her face turning a little redder with embarrassment.

"Yeah, *us*! Exactly," said Priti. "Why not try it, Zo? We'll help you. It'll be fun!"

"And you won't have to write much," said Kate.

"Plus, it's easy," Priti assured her. "Seriously. You know, my *mom* even has one, and she hates computers. So how hard could it be?"

"Let's check it out. Where's your laptop, Zo?" Kate asked Zoey, scanning the room.

Zoey pointed to her desk. Her laptop was there, buried under her stack of fashion magazines and Coco Chanel coffee table book.

Kate brought it back to the bed and lifted the

top. Zoey typed in her password and then let Priti bring up her mom's blog.

The title "Karma Mama" ran in elegant type across the top of the page. Below it was a picture of what looked like a typical, delicious dinner at the Holbrooke house.

"'Masala Mondays: Chicken Tikka Masala.'" Kate read the caption. "Yum! That looks good."

"It's a lot of Indian recipes," Priti apologized. "And the occasional story about us. *No!* Don't read it!" She grabbed Kate's hand before she could scroll down to see more pictures and posts. "It's really embarrassing."

"No, it isn't. It's awesome!" said Zoey. "You know, your mom's a great cook. I made some pancakes inspired by those coconut cardamom desserts she makes. What are those called again?"

"*Burfis?*" said Priti, shy for once.

"Well, they're my favorites! The pancake version didn't turn out so well, but that's not the point. It's really cool that she has a food blog."

"Thanks, Zoey," said Priti. "I guess it is kind of cool."

But Zoey still wasn't sure how her sketchbooks could turn into a blog.

"So you basically just follow the website's directions," Priti said. "We'll choose a blog template, scan and upload the sketches . . . type in something about them—and bam! Done."

"Fun!" said Kate. "Let's do it."

"Sure. Why not?" Zoey finally agreed. She was positive it wouldn't be as easy as Priti described, but actually, when they got started, it wasn't all that big a deal. They went to the blogging website that Priti's mom used and scrolled through pages of templates. One caught Zoey's eye right away.

"That one?" said Zoey, pointing to the screen.

"I love it! Wow, that was even easier than I thought," said Priti.

Zoey clicked on the select button. Then another window popped up asking for a name for the blog. "Oh right. We have to think of a name."

"Something catchy and simple," said Priti. "So people can remember it."

"Hmm," said Zoey, with a long, drawn-out pause. "I have no idea."

"Neither do I," said Kate.

"How about something simple, like 'Zoey's Blog'?" Zoey asked, tentatively typing it in.

"Maybe that's too simple," Priti said as she watched her. "That could be a blog about anything. Let's have fun with it and find a name that just screams 'fashion' the second you hear it."

"Good point," Zoey told her as a notice popped up. "Besides, it looks like some other Zoey with a blog already beat us to it. Okay, next?" She set her elbows in front of the keyboard and let her chin rest on her hands, then turned to Kate. "Any ideas?"

"Well . . ." Kate's smooth, tan forehead wrinkled as she tried to think. "How about . . ." She bit her lip. "No, never mind. That's silly. Mmm . . . well, how about . . ." She twirled her hair. "No, that wouldn't work. It's even worse."

Zoey sighed.

"Hey, I know!" said Priti. "How's this: 'Fashion Passion.'" She beamed. "What do you think?"

Zoey squinted. "I don't know. I get it, but it sounds kind of *intense* . . . and so not me."

"Ha!" Kate laughed. "*Sew* you! Get it? Because

you 'sew' *clothes*? Hey, maybe that's it. Sew Zoey! And spell it *s-e-w* instead of *s-o*!"

Priti's face lit up and she started nodding. She turned to Zoey to see what she thought.

Zoey cocked her head for a second. Then she grinned. "It's kind of cute."

"But wait, do you know how to sew?" Kate asked Zoey.

"Well . . . a little, but not much," Zoey said. "Not enough to make clothes like this. How cool would that be?" She pointed at a page in her sketchbook.

"No worries, Zo. You'll pick it up fast, I bet. It's the perfect name. Let's type it in," said Priti, "and hope that it's not taken yet." The girls held their breaths and crossed their fingers.

A little green light showed up next to the name "Sew Zoey."

"Got it!" yelled Kate, hugging Zoey.

"Awesome!" said Priti, jumping up and down.

The girls played around with the design a bit more, but soon the Sew Zoey blog was up for the entire world to see.

"Now you just need to upload a photo of one of

your sketches and write something," said Priti.

"Like what?" Zoey asked.

"Anything! What you think about fashion. Who you are. Why you're starting this blog."

"Okay . . ." Zoey smiled and bent over the keyboard and began to type away:

Hi, everyone! I'm Zoey—and this is . . . (drumroll, please) . . . My First Blog Post on my very first blog! As you can see, I like to draw crazy, fabulous clothes. I definitely don't consider myself a "designer"—but I hope to become one someday. That or an archeologist. Or maybe both . . . We'll see! My current fashion idols are Blake and Bauer and (of course!) Daphne Shaw, so yes, you might notice some shameless reinterpretation of past seasons now and then, I'm sure. I'm kind of (okay, very!) new at this, so bear with me while I figure it out. Though, if you're reading this, you're either (a) one of my best friends (Hi, girls!) who talked me into this and are looking over my shoulder right now or (b) someone who googled one or both of these words and got here by accident (Hi to you too!), in which case you're probably not planning to come back. But feel free to . . . I'll be here blogging and sketching and sewing! Sew long for now!

She clicked post and there it was. Up for anyone to read.

"You're funny!" Priti giggled, and then she logged Zoey out. She pulled the page back up and logged into her account. "Now *I'm* going to be your first comment," she declared with a giant grin.

Dear Sew Zoey, I love your blog! I would totally buy that dress if you made it! Keep up the good work!

"Ooh, let me add a line!" Kate said, moving in on the keyboard.

Btw, your blog name is SEW good!

"There!" Kate hit enter. Then she picked one of Zoey's sketchbooks back up. "You know, I really would wear some of these clothes if you made them. Think you could?"

"Oh, I don't think so, at least not yet." Zoey

shook her head. "I can make a skirt, *maybe*, with my aunt's help, but that's about it. . . ." Then before she knew it—without any warning at all—a lump wedged itself deep in her neck.

"What's the matter?" Kate asked quickly, reading the new look on Zoey's face. "I'm sorry. . . . What did I say?"

Zoey sighed. She wanted to answer Kate. It just wasn't an answer she wanted to talk about. Her mom was a subject she never brought up much with her friends. After all, what was there to say? Kate and Priti knew her mom was dead. It was just a fact of life—like that Kate was an only child or that Priti was Indian American.

"No, you didn't say anything wrong," said Zoey. "It's just . . . all this talk about sewing made me think about my mom. She sewed all the time. . . . She made half her clothes. And my brother's. And mine. I didn't really know her, but I miss her sometimes."

She leaned over and reached across her bed to pick up something from her nightstand. It was a photo in a frame covered with polka-dot cloth. A pretty young woman smiled out from it, holding a baby on her hip. Zoey's friends noticed two things about the pair almost right away: Their dresses matched, and even matched the fabric on the frame, and that Zoey and the woman had exactly the same smile.

"She made us matching outfits for my first birthday. See?" Zoey said.

"You look so cute!" said Priti.

"Did she make the frame too?" asked Kate. "That's so . . ." She put her hand gently on Zoey's shoulder. "That's really cool, you know?"

"I know." Zoey smiled. It really was. "It was something she loved doing . . . and I know she would have taught me a lot . . . if she were here." Zoey let out a breath. "Hey, you want to see something else?" She hadn't meant to interrupt their fun—or hers either—with such a sad subject. She carefully set the picture back down on the nightstand where it belonged. "Check this out." She slid off her bed and crossed her room to her closet and slid the doors wide apart.

"Come on." She nodded to her friends to follow,

and as they did, she pushed the carefully color-coded clothes in her closet way back to the left side of the rack. Then she reached into the right side of the closet and slid a whole other group of clothes out. "Ta-da!" she said.

"What are these?" asked Priti.

"My mom's clothes. She made them!" Zoey said. "Aren't they awesome?"

"Your mom sewed all these herself?" Kate said. Her eyes grew huge as she leaned in close. "Wow! Look at all of them."

She and Priti took in the collection, including Zoey's mother's birthday dress. There was also a flowy white sundress, a pink cardigan, paisley pants, and all sorts of other clothes. They looked like things you'd find in a really cool store—and probably spend a fortune on.

Zoey nodded. "Uh-huh. Well, not everything. Not the jeans and stuff. But a lot of it. I used to play dress up in them, but then I asked my dad last year if I could have them for real. I don't take them out that much. But just knowing they're there makes me feel, you know, in a way, that she's close. When I was little, I'd even kind of talk to them and pretend she was wearing them. I was just imagining it, but it was nice to pretend."

"Sorry, Zoey," Kate said, giving her friend's arm a squeeze.

"Me too," added Priti, but she wasn't somber for long. "If your mom could sew like this, I bet you could too."

"Really? Well, we still have her sewing machine in the basement . . . or maybe the attic. . . . I'm not sure."

"What are you waiting for?" Priti crossed her arms in front of her, as if she'd just settled the whole thing. "Start making your own clothes so you can pick up where your mom left off!"

Kate smiled at Zoey. "Yeah, you totally should," Kate told her. "Your mom would want you to, don't you think?"

Zoey started to shrug, but as the question sank in, a happy tingle made her nod. "Maybe . . . yeah, she probably would. Okay." Just thinking about it made her smile.

The next morning, after Kate and Priti went home, Zoey found her dad in the garage stretching before his five-mile Sunday jog.

"Hey, Dad?"

"Hey, hon. What's up? Did your friends already go home?"

Zoey nodded. "Yeah. Thanks for letting them stay over. I hope we didn't keep you up."

"Me?" He shook his head. "Nah. But I am sorry they couldn't stay for our secret-ingredient pancakes. What should we put in them today?"

The pancakes had been a Sunday tradition for years now, ever since they got the idea from Zoey's favorite cooking show (at the time). She and her dad would make the batter and pick out a secret ingredient to spice them up . . . then they'd serve them to Marcus, whose challenge was to guess what was inside. Sometimes it was easy, like chocolate chips or bananas or crushed Oreos (yum!). But lately Zoey had been trying things like candied ginger with peaches on top or those toasted coconut with cardamom pancakes inspired by Priti's mom's dessert. That one had really stumped

Marcus: He guessed buttermilk, sour cream, cinnamon, clove, and caramel before finally giving up . . . and digging in.

"I don't know, Dad. . . . Do we have any ricotta?"

He nodded. "I think we might."

"That, with some lemon zest . . ."

"*Mmm.* A classic." He winked. "Sounds good! So, like I said, what's up, Zo?" he went on, grinning. "Wanna join me for a run?"

"Uh, no." Zoey shook her head as her dad's hopeful grin turned into a playful pout. She nodded to the heart-covered boxers that she'd slept in and the flip-flops she'd put on to walk outside.

Her dad chuckled and went back to stretching. "Okay, well, maybe next time."

"I actually had a question for you, Dad. I was wondering—" She stopped, and without even thinking she swallowed the question back down. She'd rehearsed it a dozen times in her head, but it was suddenly a whole different thing trying to get it out. What if she broke her mother's precious machine? What if mentioning it made her dad sad?

Her dad, meanwhile, crossed his arms as worry

rearranged his face. "Go on. What happened . . . ?" Then he got a little twinkle in his eye. "Does a boy want to take you to a movie or something? I thought we had a few years before that stuff."

What?

"No!"

Zoey closed her eyes and actually felt her ears turn red. The very idea her dad had gone there made her want to evaporate right then.

"Well, what?" her dad prompted.

Zoey opened one eye and decided to just say it before he came up with something even more insane and embarrassing. "Can I . . . could I . . . may I use Mom's sewing machine, Dad? Please? I promise I'll be very careful. But I totally understand if you say no. It's just . . . I think I might like to make clothes . . . like she did . . . and I think I'm old enough. . . ."

She looked at her dad, and he looked at her, and before she knew it, she was wrapped in his arms.

"Honey, I think that's a great idea," he said. "It's time that thing stopped collecting dust."

CHAPTER 4

Sew Cool!

So who knew that blogging would be so much fun? I might like it as much as I love polka dots, which is a LOT. Polka dots just make me happy, you know? So, in honor of National Polka-Dot Day (which I think I just made up), I'm attaching a drawing of a polka-dot dress and an outfit with a similar pattern of hearts and stars instead of dots. What do you think?

But as much as I like polka dots and showing you my drawings, virtual clothes just aren't as much fun as real clothes—at all! So, I've decided to start sewing. Small hitch in the plan: The most complicated thing I've sewed myself is a tote bag I decorated with fabric paint at day camp a million years ago. (Okay, okay, it was two years ago!) I'm going to use Mom's sewing machine tomorrow, but I thought I'd practice with a good old-fashioned needle and thread tonight, just to get in the sewing mood. Dad's thrilled. . . . He said if I'm sewing, I might as well sew buttons on some of the shirts that have been stuck in laundry purgatory for ages. . . .

But I'm not exaggerating when I tell you that I prick my fingers every time I try to sew. Every. Single. Time. I think the only solution is to buy TEN thimbles and wear one on each finger. Problem solved, right?

The thing is, this is hard. Harder than I thought it would be. And they're just buttons! I know my mom loved sewing, so I'm hoping it's in my genes . . . Get it? In my "jeans"? Shameless fashion-pun alert! It's cheesy,

I know, but it's my blog and I'll pun if I want to. So, on that note, I'm going to get back to sewing. Well, sort of. Wish me luck!

Sure enough, the sewing machine was in the basement, and as soon as he got back from running on Sunday, Zoey's dad brought it up. There wasn't really a place in Zoey's room to put it, so it went on the dining room table instead.

"Are you sure it's okay here?" Zoey asked her dad, even though they never used the room.

He nodded and smiled the half smile that went with thoughts of Zoey's mom. "Oh yeah," he told Zoey. "It's where it always used to go."

Zoey followed the directions for how to thread the machine, or tried to, but it was really complicated. She did the best she could and then got up to find some fabric to sew.

In the linen closet, Zoey found an ancient, fraying sheet that she knew nobody would miss. She folded it in half and slid it under the presser foot of the machine—the part that looked like a little ski.

Okay, it's go time, she thought. She gave the foot pedal a tap and the machine whirred instantly to life . . . and then choked to death just as fast, making an awful crunching sound.

Uh-oh! What was that?

Zoey was sure that she had broken it, but after she pulled out a wad of tangled thread, everything seemed to be okay. Still, when she gave it one more shot, the exact same thing happened again. Plus, when she looked at the fabric, there weren't any stitches in it.

"That doesn't sound good," said Zoey's brother, Marcus.

"This really isn't as easy as it looks," Zoey said, discouraged. In fact, it wasn't easy at all, and Zoey decided it was time to call for reinforcements. She grabbed her cell phone and dialed the number of the only person she knew who could help.

"Hi, Aunt Lulu? I have a fashion emergency," Zoey said as she slumped miserably before the machine. "Any chance you could help me learn how to sew ?"

On Monday at Camp Lulu, Zoey had a crash course in Sewing 101. Aunt Lulu started with teaching Zoey how to thread the machine for real.

"You have to loop the bobbin thread onto the needle thread first," said Aunt Lulu.

"Oh right!" Zoey said. "That would help!"

Things went much better after that.

Aunt Lulu tossed a bag of fabric swatches onto the table. "Let's start with the basics," she told Zoey. "Sewing two pieces of fabric together by stitching in a straight line."

"Okay," Zoey said. She picked up a few swatches, and Aunt Lulu helped her pin them together and slide them between the presser foot and the throat plate.

"Ready to give it a go?" she asked. "You don't have to pull the fabric through. This thingamajig moves it along while you press the foot pedal. It's called a 'feed dog,' I think. "

"Feed dog, really? That's a funny name," said Zoey, with an amused look. "Are you sure you aren't making it up?"

"Not really," said Aunt Lulu, cracking a smile.

"But it's so odd it must be true, right? Okay, give it a whirl!"

Zoey sat down and placed her foot on the pedal that made the machine run, holding the fabric down with her hands. *Okay, this is it,* she thought, giving herself a pep talk. *Ready, set, sew!*

She started off pressing on the pedal very lightly.

It was so light that nothing happened.

Then she tried pressing a little harder, stopping and starting to see what the thread was doing. The machine jerked along.

"Try to keep the speed at a steady pace, Zo. It just takes practice," Aunt Lulu told Zoey.

Zoey pressed her foot down firmly this time. The needle whirred up and down until she could hardly see it, and the fabric raced through the machine in a blur.

She tried to stop, but it was too late. The line of stitches ran right off the edge of the fabric.

"Whoa, there," said Aunt Lulu. "A little less gas next time."

"Oops!" said Zoey. Her heart was racing. It took her a second to work up the courage to look at the fabric. When she did, there was a mostly straight line of stitches. "Hey, look at that! The stiches look pretty good, right?" She paused and squinted a little. "Something's off, though. What is it?"

Aunt Lulu laughed. "Now it's my turn for an 'oops'! I forgot to tell you about seam guides," she said. She pointed to the little lines etched in the throat plate of the machine. "Next time try to look at these lines while you sew. They help you keep the stitches straight *and* parallel to the edge of the fabric."

"Gotcha," Zoey said. "I'll just try that again."

Soon Zoey mastered sewing in a straight line and moved on to the backstitch.

"So, you just sew back and forth over the first and last few stitches to keep them from unraveling, like tying a knot when you sew by hand," Aunt Lulu explained.

"Cool! What's next?"

"Hmm, I'm not sure. You know, I'm pretty rusty," Aunt Lulu said. "Your grandma taught me and your mom to sew when we were little, but I haven't sewn actual *clothes* in ages. Your mom was the seamstress in the family. She had the patience for sewing dresses," she remembered fondly. "I stick to simple things, like drapes and pillows."

"Ooh! Can I make a pillow?" Zoey asked.

"You know, that's a great project to start with."

Aunt Lulu had a closet full of fabric samples and let Zoey pick some out. Zoey settled on a print with pink and orange stars to make into a pillow for her desk chair.

She cut two matching squares out of the cloth and pinned it along the edges, then she started to sew up one side. It went so smoothly and so quickly that before she knew it, she'd stitched up all four sides.

"That's going to be hard to stuff now," her aunt gently teased. "But I guess that's what seam rippers are for, right? We'll fix this in a jiffy."

She quickly opened up the seam and showed Zoey how to add buttonholes along the side. Still, it seemed like it needed something else. . . .

"Hey! I have an idea," Zoey said. "Can I have some white fabric? I'm going to stitch a *Z* for Zoey on the front."

"Perfect!" said Aunt Lulu. "Then we just need some buttons and batting to stuff it with. . . ." She grabbed her car keys. "To the fabric store!"

Zoey had seen A Stitch in Time before at the shopping center, but she'd never been inside. All she could think when she stepped through the doors was, *Where has this place been all my life?*

It was as big as a supermarket, but instead of aisles full of food, there were rows and rows of fabric bolts. She took a deep breath. It had a *smell* . . . like a pet store or a pizza place has a smell you instantly know. This place had one that was cool and clean and new and full of ideas. Zoey breathed in again. *Possibility!* That's what the smell was!

Up at the front were calicos for quilting and prints with characters, like talking bugs and princesses. Then came the good stuff—silk, satin, wool and corduroy, velvet, denim, flannel and fleece, fluffy tulle and delicate lace, plus a whole section full of fur and feathers, which were clearly and fabulously fake.

And then, *then* came the whole wall full of

buttons . . . How was she ever going to pick out one kind? She was drawn at once to the ones that looked like enormous jewels . . . but then there were some that were shaped like daisies, and frogs, and fish, and even *skulls*. She wanted them all! At last, she settled on big, sparkly stars made out of rhinestones. On the way down the aisle she passed the wall of ribbons and tassels and zippers. She could hardly look. They were so pretty, they made her eyes hurt.

Her aunt, meanwhile, quickly located the aisle with batting, then found Zoey and followed her hungry gaze around the store. "You know, while we're here," she said, "we should pick out a pattern, so you can make something else. Don't you think, Zo?"

Zoey's face broke into a wide grin, which was an answer and then some.

The pattern books were laid out on a tall U of counters in the middle of the store. They were as big and heavy as paving stones, and several times as thick.

"Let's start with something for beginners," said

Aunt Lulu as she lifted a book's glossy cover and opened it to the E-Z tab.

There seemed to be a little of everything, Zoey thought as she browsed. There were patterns for skirts and tops and dresses and even a doggie raincoat. . . .

"Looking for anything special?"

Zoey looked up to see an older woman with long, jet-black hair. She was wearing a green leopard-print blouse that tied at the neck and a blue skirt.

"Not really . . . ," Zoey answered.

Aunt Lulu put her hand on Zoey's shoulder. "My niece is just learning to sew," she explained. "So we'd like to find something easy."

"Ah!" The woman rubbed her hands together. "Then you've come to the right place!" A pair of rainbow-striped reading glasses dangled from a beaded chain around her neck. She slipped them on and peered down at the pattern page.

"This book is good," she said. "But I have another one. Wait right here." She spun around and heaved another book off the counter behind them and lugged it over to where Zoey stood.

"Now . . ." The woman opened it. "I'm assuming you want a pattern size that would fit you? I took the liberty of grabbing a petites pattern book. Those should fit you pretty well, at your height."

"Ooh, these look good!" Zoey exclaimed. On the very first page she saw the cutest pajama pants. If she got right to work, she thought, maybe she could wear them to bed that night!

A few pages later there was a picture that immediately caught her eye: beach cover-ups. She needed one. And so did Priti and Kate!

"Now, those are cute!" said Zoey. "Maybe I can make some for my best friends too. We're around the same height. Well, Kate's a little taller."

"That's a great idea! And it should fit your friends too. It's a forgiving cut," the woman agreed. "You know, you could make that one out of terry cloth—or even a nice woven cotton."

Zoey nodded. "Maybe I could also mix it up. You know? Do a little of both?"

The woman turned to her, grinning, and tilted her head back a few degrees. "What's your name, sweetheart?" she asked Zoey.

"Zoey."

"I'm Jan," said the woman. "And I can tell already that I like you a whole lot, and I like your style, too." She slid her glasses down her nose and eyed Zoey up and down, nodding in approval of her gray collared sleeveless top, red ruffled skirt, and orange Converse. "I have an idea for how to pull it all together." Then she ran over to the wall of ribbons and snipped a short length of minty green silk ribbon.

"May I?" Jan asked, pointing at Zoey's collar. Zoey nodded, and Jan tied the ribbon around her neck in a pretty bow. "There. The finishing touch, I think. Or you could use the ribbon as a headband, if that's more your thing."

"Very nice!" said Aunt Lulu.

"Wow," said Zoey as she glanced at the mirror and then back at Jan with a big smile on her face. The ribbon really did pull everything together. She never would have thought of that! Zoey wasn't quite sure what to say, but Jan didn't seem to mind. She shut the pattern books decisively and took Zoey's hand in hers.

"You just wait here," she told Aunt Lulu. "I'm going to take good care of your niece."

Zoey grinned and waved good-bye to her aunt as she trotted off with Jan.

"This is where the magic happens," Jan said when they came to a long row of metal drawers. They held all the actual patterns, she told Zoey, and she showed her how to use the numbers from the books to find the ones she wanted to make.

Then it was off to the maze of fabrics, which Jan knew like the back of her hand. She steered Zoey away from the pricey designer silks ("thirty dollars a yard") and to simpler cottons and jerseys ("so much easier to sew with—and to wash"), and before Zoey knew it, she had yards of material.

Jan even threw in an armful of remnants—leftover pieces that were too small to sell. "I know you'll do something divine with these. Just promise to show me what you make," she said.

Still, by the time the notions were added—which was a word Zoey learned meant everything from thread to buttons to trim—Aunt Lulu and Zoey's little shopping trip had become expensive.

"Uh-oh . . . ," said Zoey when the grand total was tallied.

She looked at Aunt Lulu, who took out her wallet and shrugged.

"Looks like you'll be dog-sitting for me for the rest of your life, huh?" she said. "Don't worry, Zoey, it's my treat."

------- CHAPTER 5 -------

My Sewing Saga

Beware, whoever is out there reading this, I might have to change the name of this blog from "Sew Zoey" to "Not Sew Zoey" if my sewing skills don't improve soon. My Sewing Saga goes like this: It started yesterday, when I discovered my own slice of heaven, a.k.a. better than Disneyland, a.k.a. Willy Wonka's Fabric Factory. Did you guess? (Spoiler alert: My aunt took me to the fabric store.) I've never seen so many pretty things in one place! I also got a nice vocab lesson—the sewing word of the day is "notions." I wonder who came up with that one!

Then, when I got home from the store, I started working on a project. The thing is, I accidentally sewed the shirt I was WEARING to the skirt I was trying to make. (Thanks, Aunt Lulu, for telling me to tuck in my shirt next time!) And that's not all: I just accidentally destroyed my bedspread cutting some fabric for some extremely cute— (Oops! I almost forgot! They're surprises. Never mind! Moving on!) Anyhoo, let this be a lesson to any aspiring fashion designers out there: Do not, I repeat, do not, under any circumstances cut out patterns on your bed (like I did)! Trust me, it's a Fashion Emergency just waiting to happen.

On the other hand, the bedspread is (was?) kind of awesome. Maybe I can salvage the material so it isn't a complete waste. I'm totally channeling Maria from *The Sound of Music*, right? When she made outfits for the von Trapp family out of old curtains? All I can say is

I'm going to be wearing a lot of stripes this year! Stay tuned, fashion fans. . . . And while you're waiting, check out my latest sketches: a button dress and a chalkboard dress that could be written on in chalk!

PS For inspiration, I just re-watched the greatest documentary ever about Daphne Shaw, my favorite designer and sewing genius. (If you haven't seen it, promise you will! It's amazing.)

"There you are!"

"What took you so long?"

Kate ran up with Priti and they both greeted Zoey with a warm, chlorinated hug. They'd been waiting for her impatiently outside the girls' dressing room at the pool. Zoey hugged them back, squinting as her eyes adjusted to the sun.

Priti, meanwhile, took a second to stroke the sleeve of Zoey's cover-up. "This is so cute!"

Kate cocked her head. "It looks familiar. . . ."

Priti clapped. "Oh! I know where it's from! I read your blog this morning."

Zoey blushed.

"It's from your bedspread! Gosh! You mean you made it?" Kate twirled her finger as a signal for Zoey to turn around. "What'd your dad say?"

"He was just glad I didn't cut myself," Zoey said, relieved. "So, what do you think?" she asked, doing another little twirl.

Priti crossed her arms. "It's adorable! I love it! I can't believe you made that."

"I can't either," Zoey said. "You know, I never thought I'd love sewing this much. The other night I was so focused on making this work that I completely forgot to watch the new episode of *Fashion Showdown*."

"Oh, it was a really good one too!" Priti said. "Let me know when you're caught up so we can talk about it."

Zoey really had been sewing all the time for the last few weeks. She would text her friends with pictures of her latest creations—and they were also *reading* all about them on Sew Zoey every day. They loved how excited she was, but they also missed hanging out with her, and she could tell. She missed them too. After all, school would be starting soon,

and the countdown to the end of summer had offi-
cially begun.

"I'm glad you took a break to come to the pool!"
Kate said.

"I know, I'm sorry I've been MIA," Zoey said.
"But I promise I'll make the next few weeks count.
Plus, I have a surprise for you. . . ."

She reached into the tote bag on her shoulder and
took out two neatly folded bundles. She hoped they
would help her friends realize she hadn't forgotten
them while she was busy blogging and sewing. She
handed one to Priti and the other one to Kate and
waited while they unwrapped the packages.

"Whoa!" Kate gasped as she realized that it was
a cover-up too. "Did you make this for me?"

It was the same simple minidress style as Zoey's,
but the resemblance pretty much ended there.
Zoey's was made out of the pink-and-white-striped
bedspread fabric, with the stripes going vertically
in the middle and horizontal on the sides. Kate's,
on the other hand, had a red terry-cloth body and
three silver racing stripes going down each side.

"Do you like it?" Zoey asked her. "I made it the

colors of the swim team so if you wanted to, you could wear it to swim meets."

"I know!" Kate said. "I love it!"

Zoey turned to Priti, who was admiring her own cover-up, which looked completely different, even though it was the same shape. Priti's was made out of a semi-sheer turquoise fabric with not one or two but *three* layers of matching fringe along the hem. Priti held it up by the shoulders and gave it a little shake. Then she slipped it over her head and wiggled her hips.

"Thank you, Zoey! It's *amazing*!"

"Do you forgive me?" Zoey asked.

"Yes! Totally!" Priti and Kate said, giving Zoey hugs.

Then Priti added, "As long as you'll forgive us for sometimes giving you a hard time for sewing so much. We just missed seeing you."

Kate put her cover-up on too, and they started across the concrete deck.

"We saved some chairs in the good corner," said Priti, pointing to the primo spot near the deep end. Not only did the chairs face north instead of into the sun, they were far from the kiddie pool—a.k.a. "no-man's land."

"Oh good," said Zoey, looking around. "Wow, it's crowded today, huh?"

She hadn't been to the pool in more than two weeks. She'd wanted to come last weekend, but both days there were thunderstorms. In the end, though, she hadn't minded because it meant she could stay home—and sew and design clothes to her heart's content. That was when she'd worked on the surprises for Priti and Kate.

Zoey had always loved the pool. But this summer was different. Zoey and her friends were getting too old to play Marco Polo or Sharks and Minnows in the shallow end now—and yet, every forty-five minutes, they still had to climb out of the deep end for "adult swim." Days at the pool felt hot . . . and slow.

It was different for Kate, who had her swim team friends. And for Priti too, who never got tired of reading and was even known to take her book into the pool. They also didn't seem as bothered by something else that, for Zoey, had started to take some fun out of the scene: the whole parading-around-in-a-bathing-suit thing. *Ugh!* Honestly, she'd rather wear her old uniform than a bathing suit—even a one-piece. For that reason too her brand-new cover-up was a truly marvelous thing.

"Excuse me, girls?"

Zoey and her friends turned to see a young woman with huge, glamorous sunglasses looking up from her lounge chair.

"Yes?" They looked at one another, then back at the lady. Was she talking to them?

"I just had to ask you. . . ." She slid her sunglasses up and perched them on the top of her glossy red hair. "Where did you get those adorable cover-ups? They're fabulous!" she said.

The girls looked at one another again, this time stifling laughs.

"Oh, these?" Priti tossed her hair back and shifted her shoulders to make her fringe sway. "*These* were custom made for us."

Kate and Zoey laughed a little bit until they saw the woman's expression. She didn't realize Priti was being silly.

"What a shame," said the woman, sighing as she pulled her sunglasses back down.

"Actually, it's amazing," Kate said. "*She* made them." She pointed to Zoey, who began to blush.

"Really?" They could see the woman's brows jump from surprise behind her glasses. "Wow!" She crossed her arms in front of her metallic bikini top. "You are so talented!"

"Thanks!" said Zoey. She gave her friends a wide-eyed look that said *can you believe this is really happening?* and then followed their lead as they continued toward their chairs.

TWWWEEEEEEEEEEE!!!! Suddenly the blast of a whistle shot down from the lifeguard stand. Zoey looked up to see her brother, Marcus, standing up from his chair. He was aiming both pointer fingers at a boy who looked about six. "You're benched!" he shouted at him, letting his whistle fall to his chest. "Yes, *you*," he went on as the boy looked innocently around. "I saw you push that girl. Twenty minutes on the deck."

Marcus's Ray-Bans followed the boy as he climbed out of the water and sat down by his mother. Zoey couldn't tell if Marcus had seen her. Her brother was fine when they were home—probably better than the average brother, in fact. But now that he was a lifeguard, he was—to put it mildly—utterly oblivious to her. He took his first job really seriously and always kept his eyes on the pool. Sometimes Zoey wondered if people who didn't know them would even guess that they were related, let alone siblings.

They did look alike. They both had the same dark brown hair and the same hazel eyes. Hers were a little greener, though. His were a little more gold. And they both had the same dimpled smiles, but now that he was so tan, his teeth seemed twice as bright. Where Marcus had their dad's thick, line-straight eyebrows, however, and his angular nose, Zoey had her mom's softer features and—well-hidden—cheekbones.

"C'mon." Priti grabbed Zoey's hand and pulled her forward around the diving board.

"Hold up," said Kate, sounding panicked. "Where did our stuff go? I thought it was on those chairs over there."

Priti dropped Zoey's hand and crossed her arms. "It *was* on those chairs," she said.

Zoey's eyes followed Kate's and Priti's to the three chairs at the end of the row—and the three girls lying in them: Ivy Wallace and her sidekicks for the past year, Bree Sharpe and Shannon Chang.

Ivy, Bree, and Shannon all went to Mapleton Prep too. Zoey and Shannon met in the third grade and had even been friends for a while, or so Zoey thought. But that was history once middle school started. Shannon joined up with Ivy and Bree, who had gone to a different elementary school, and she was different with them. Zoey had tried to be welcoming to Ivy and Bree. She learned pretty fast, though, that Ivy Wallace wasn't the kind of girl she wanted as a friend. Once, Zoey and Bree were paired up as lab partners—which had gone fine until Ivy sent Bree a note. Then Bree folded up her own lab notes and gave them to Ivy, so she could have them, and Bree had to start over from the beginning. Zoey wanted nothing to do with that kind of thing. And she knew she was lucky Priti and Kate would never cheat.

"Excuse us," Priti said as she, Kate, and Zoey lined up at the foot of the hijacked chairs.

Ivy looked up and pulled out an earbud.

"Oh, hi, Priti," said Ivy. "What's up?"

"Uh, what's up, Ivy, is that you're in *our* chairs," she said.

"*Your* chairs? I don't understand," Ivy said. She turned to Bree and Shannon, who each set their phones down and looked at Ivy, nodding to back her up. Then Ivy tossed her hair back, trying not to blink in the sun.

"Oh, come on, Ivy," Kate spoke up. "What'd you do with our stuff? We left towels right here, along with our bags."

Ivy shrugged. "I don't know. . . . Do you mean that junk over there? Is that *yours*?"

Ivy pointed to the three last lounge chairs in the row by the chain link fence—all the way back in no-man's-land. Sure enough, there lay Kate's and Priti's towels and bags.

"Um, excuse me! It's not junk," Priti replied. "It's our stuff."

"Sorry, it looked like junk to me," Ivy went on,

knitting her eyebrows with fake concern.

"Yeah, me too," said Shannon.

"You know, that's why I never leave my stuff hanging around," Ivy said. Her eyes flew up to the lifeguard stand and settled on Marcus. "Especially when my stuff's by the *cute* lifeguard."

Cute lifeguard . . . ? Who?

Then Zoey realized Ivy didn't know that the "cute lifeguard" was Zoey's brother. All three of them stood there, fists clenched. Zoey's tongue was clenched as well—and itching to spring. She glanced back at the lifeguard stand and saw that Marcus was on a break and another lifeguard was on duty.

"Speaking of lifeguards . . . ," said Zoey. "I think I'll tell him what you did. . . ." She turned and waved to Marcus. "Yoo-hoo! Lifeguard! Excuse me!" she yelled, praying he wouldn't ignore her this time.

She heard Ivy snort behind her. "Seriously? You're just making a fool of yourself. As if he really cares."

"Oh, believe me, he cares," said Zoey.

"You're dreaming," said Ivy. Then her smug smile

turned into a confused stare as Marcus walked over and stopped to give Zoey a high five.

"Hey, sis," Marcus said, oblivious to what was going on. "What's up? Are these your friends?" He nodded toward Ivy, Bree, and Shannon.

"Hey, Marcus." She paused to enjoy Ivy's horrified expression. "Nope. Not really."

"OMG, we're totally friends," Ivy said. "We just invited Zoey and . . . those girls . . . to sit with us. Here, take our seats."

"Actually, they took our—" continued Zoey.

"What? No! No! No! . . . That was a total joke. You can't take things so *seriously*!" Ivy blurted, stumbling to her feet. She avoided catching Zoey's eye and made sure to flash a smile at Marcus. "Everything's good, Zoey, right?"

Zoey crossed her arms and looked up. She wasn't ready to say quite yet. . . .

"Here, I promise, they're all yours," huffed Ivy, pointing at the chairs. "Shannon! Go get their stuff already, and bring it back over here."

While Shannon's mouth fell open and Bree looked like she wanted to disappear into the pool deck, Zoey grinned at Priti and Kate. Then Zoey looked back to Marcus, who mouthed, *Are you okay?*

I am now, thanks! Zoey mouthed back, smiling, while she and her friends waited for the lounge squatters to finish clearing out.

"Here, let me help," Ivy told Shannon, loud enough so Marcus could hear her. "I'd do *anything* for Zoey!"

Before they could reclaim their seats completely, though, a stereo of voices shouted out Priti's name.

"Hey, Priti! Zoey! Kate!" It was Priti's sisters and one of their friends, waving from a cluster of chairs behind the diving board. "You guys want to sit here? We're getting up to leave."

Priti spun around and waved back. "Oh good! Those chairs are even better!" she said.

By the time they got there, Sashi and Tara were up with their bags on their shoulders and their sandals on their feet. Their friend had out her cars keys and was balancing a stack of glossy magazines.

"Do you guys want these? I'm done," she said.

"Sure!" said Zoey hungrily.

"Of course she does," said Sashi. "Hey, you know who this is," she told her friend.

"Who?" said the girl. She was wearing a white two-piece and an aqua sarong.

"It's Priti's friend, the Sew Zoey blogger!" Sashi told her.

"Wow!" said her friend. "Cool! Sew Zoey. I love that blog!" She pointed her keys at Zoey's cover-up. "Don't tell me you made *that*."

Zoey nodded, biting her lip to keep her smile contained.

"Yep! And these too." Priti spoke up, pointing to hers and Kate's.

"Wow. And you're still in middle school? I really thought you'd be older," said the girl, raising her eyebrows approvingly.

Zoey wanted to run up and hug her, but she kept it to a modest nod. *Too bad Ivy missed that!* she thought.

"We all love your blog," Tara told her. "And we've been telling *all* our friends."

"Did you tell Annika?" her friend asked her.

"Of course," Tara replied. "She's our friend who's

interning in New York," she informed Zoey. She reached for one of the magazines and held it up. "For this."

Whoa, thought Zoey. *Très Chic!* It was only the most famous fashion magazine in the whole, entire world! The very thought of someone even remotely connected to it reading her blog gave Zoey goose bumps all over.

And now she finally knew where at least some of her blog's new followers were coming from. At the same time, though, she was instantly nervous at the thought of all those eyes looking at her drawings and reading her blog posts. It was one thing to do something for herself and her friends . . . but it was another to do something for strangers. Strangers who would judge her by her blog and her blog alone.

"It was so cool to meet you," said Priti's sisters' friend as they waved and started off. "I can't wait to read your next post—and to hear what you decide to make for the first day of school!"

Zoey sighed and sank into her chaise without even laying down her towel first. Ivy, Shannon, and Bree? Who were they again? And who ever said the pool wasn't great? It was totally awesome! Too bad summer was almost over.

"So!" Priti adjusted her chair, so that it didn't lean so far back. She had her book open, at the ready, in the middle of her lap. "What *are* you making, Zoey? Have you started on it yet?"

"Not yet," said Zoey. "I've got a bunch of ideas, though. Did you see the ones I posted?"

"Of course," Kate said. "That 'Ode to Mrs. Hammerfall' look was hilarious!"

Priti giggled. "How funny would it be," she said, "if we *all* went to the first day of school in turtlenecks and pleated pants! I dare you!"

Kate doubled over, howling in laughter, and Zoey did too. They were totally aware that half the pool was staring at them, but they didn't care.

"Seriously," Zoey said finally. "No, seriously, guys! Which outfit did you like?"

Kate dried her eyes with the hem of her cover-up. "That chalkboard dress was really cool."

Priti nodded. "Ooh, yeah, I liked that too."

"If only they made chalkboard material . . . ," said Zoey. "Maybe I can use chalkboard paint."

"Or the dress made of ties," said Priti. "Maybe go with something like that."

"Do you have enough ties?" asked Kate.

Zoey laughed. "Oh, you haven't seen my dad's closet," she said. "Plus, they're ten for a dollar at the thrift store. The hard part is sewing them all together. . . . The orange skirt might be more fun, anyway. *Ugh!*" Zoey threw back her head and let out a groan.

"What?" Kate and Priti both asked.

"This back-to-school thing. It just hit me that it's coming so fast. There's so much more I want to do. . . ."

Priti sighed and looked at Kate and put her book down next to her. She took Zoey's hand and pulled her up. "Come. You need a dip in the pool!" she said.

---------- CHAPTER 6 ----------

Back to School

The last few weeks of summer were a total blur. What happened? Now it's the night before school and my big debut. So here it is: the back-to-school look that you, the Sew Zoey followers, voted on. . . . And while I hate to state the obvious, bravo, guys! You have excellent taste, if I say so myself. You totally chose my favorite combination! I'd be happy to never see my old uniform again, but it's kind of cool to "reclaim" that old tie and give it a new, fashionable life. (I believe in English last year, Mrs. Gimmel called it "appropriation." See, Mrs. G.? I was paying attention, after all.)

So now that the outfit is all figured out, I have a confession to make: I, all of a sudden, got seriously crazy-jittery about tomorrow. I've had a bunch of first days before—first day of camp, first day of kindergarten, etc.—but this first day is freaking me out a little. It's the first day of a really big first impression. I don't usually care so much what the other kids think, but really, deep down, I hope they like the outfit as much as you do. Is that silly? Anyway, thanks for listening/reading/whatever.

Okay! Ten hours to fashion liftoff and counting . . . Wish me luck!

Zoey stood in front of her mirror inspecting her outfit for the umtillionth time. The problem was, the more she looked, the more sick her stomach felt. She was just realizing something that morning that anyone who'd ever lived to tell the tale about middle school should have known: Styling the perfect look was one thing . . . but actually *wearing* it to Mapleton Prep on the first day of school was something else.

Where were all those Sew Zoey followers right now when she really needed them? she thought. Where was Coco24/7 to tell her that making a skirt with the seams inside out was truly inspired? Where was Fashionsista to push her to keep practicing pleating until she got the hang of it for next time? Where were Kate and Priti, for that matter, to remind her it was *she*, after all, who started the petition to get rid of school uniforms?

Right now it was just Zoey and the mirror, and neither one was saying much. Instead, nerve-racking thoughts filled Zoey's head. Thoughts, specifically, about Ivy Wallace and all the other people like her at school. There weren't a lot of them, thank goodness. But it didn't take more than one to ruin your whole day. And while Zoey hadn't had any more run-ins at the pool with Ivy and her crew, she knew it was mostly because Marcus was there and Ivy seemed to be under the delusion that she had a chance with him. At school, there'd be no Marcus to bring out her fake, friendly side.

"Zoey, honey, you're going to miss the bus!" Dad's voice shot straight through Zoey's door from the base of the stairs.

"I'm *coming*," she called. "Just a sec."

She took a deep breath to calm the butterflies in her stomach, then squared her shoulders and inventoried her outfit once again.

Tie belt? Check.

Orange skirt with inside-out seams? Check.

Turquoise top? Check

Polka-dotted leggings? Check.

Marcus's old high-tops? Check.

Purple shoelaces? Check.

Crippling doubts and anxiety? Check and *double* check.

Bam-bam. A fist drummed on her door, and Zoey opened it with a sigh.

"Hey, Zo, I just wanted to say bye, I'm off. Good luck at school to— *Whoa*."

Marcus's face froze for a second in a complicated

combo of surprise and disbelief. He started to say something, then he stopped. He cocked his head to the side and pointed at her outfit.

"School?"

Zoey nodded. "Uh-huh. First day of no uniforms. So I made it, um, myself."

"Wow." He nodded back, though he still didn't quite seem to understand.

"Is it that bad? I look like a freak, don't I?" muttered Zoey. She fiddled with the belt.

"What? *No.*" Marcus shook his head. "You look awesome," he told her. "I mean, I'm no fashion expert or anything, but I think you look totally cool . . . and totally you."

"So, you don't think I'll stand out too much?"

"Uh, no." Marcus exhaled a laugh. "I didn't say *that.*"

"*Ohhh . . .*" Zoey hung her head.

"But hey, who cares?" Marcus went on. "Who said there's anything wrong with standing out?"

"Nobody," mumbled Zoey, remembering how she'd said practically the same thing to Priti and Kate. "I'm just not used to doing it at school."

"Well, maybe you should get used to it," he replied bluntly. "Hey, are those my old shoes?"

Zoey looked up and started to smile just as Marcus's phone buzzed in his hand. He looked down. "Oh, gotta run. Sorry, Zo. James is giving me a ride, and he's waiting out front." He turned and made for the stairs, then for a split second he spun back around. "Hey, Zo, if you're not comfortable, change. But don't do it for anyone but yourself."

Zoey watched him go, and she couldn't help thinking how great her brother was, as far as brothers go. Of course, it was easy for someone who looked like him to say "just be yourself." He could probably wear a bathrobe to school and no one would say a thing.

Zoey was proud of the clothes she made and was honestly a little excited to show them off. But was she completely comfortable actually wearing them? Not so much. At least not today.

Suddenly Zoey knew what she needed. She moved toward her closet and solemnly slid the doors apart. Then she reached for the hangers that she kept way, way back, out of sight.

"Hi, Mom," Zoey said softly. "I wish you were here. I mean, I wish you were here all the time . . . but especially today. And I was thinking I could borrow something of yours for good luck."

There! She spotted a cardigan on one of the hangers. It was pink and slightly frayed. Zoey recognized it from pictures of her mom in art school. It had a few splotches of paint and smears of bright pastels—as if she wore it all the time. And when Zoey slipped it on over her shirt, she felt like she was getting a big hug.

Then she looked in the mirror again.

And this time she smiled back. It was the perfect finishing touch.

"*Zoey!*"

"Coming, Dad!" she called.

Her dad was standing there by the front door with a cold pancake in his hand. His eyes popped the instant he saw her, and his eyebrows slid up his forehead. Zoey stopped on the stairs and raised her chin and put her hands on her hips.

"Well, what do you think?"

Her dad's eyes darted across her outfit until

they landed on her mom's cardigan. His eyes softened and he smiled. "You look great. Really great, Zo, honey."

The first test, thought Zoey, would be the bus. She held her breath as she climbed on. She waited for the first stinging comments . . . but surprisingly, they didn't come. Instead, she got a smile from Ms. Stern, the bus driver, who was anything *but* stern. She was dressed up herself for the first day of school in what looked like a brand-new T-shirt from her summer vacation in Maine. It was white and had a big red lobster on it and said I (LOBSTER) MAINE with a lobster where the heart would go.

"Liking this no-more-uniform thing, huh, Zoey?" Ms. Stern grinned. "Looking good!"

"Thanks!" Zoey told her. "You too!"

The driver waved her back and Zoey hurried to take a seat, and *still*, Zoey couldn't believe it, there wasn't a peep. No looks. No giggles. No swiveling stares. Just five boys with their heads bowed down intently over their phones, playing games. And that was it until Kate hopped on at the next stop, two blocks away. Zoey was way too surprised at *Kate's* outfit, however, to even talk about her own.

"What happened to the stuff you got?" asked Zoey.

Instead of the dress Zoey had found for Kate at the mall, Kate was wearing a plain white shirt with a little embroidery on the neckline.

"And the jeans?" Zoey eyed Kate's blue Bermuda shorts.

"What can I say? My mom didn't think they were 'appropriate' for the first day, and you know I can't argue with her. But look!" Kate lifted a foot to show off her new tan-and-blue skater shoes. "I'm wearing those shoes that you like. See?"

Zoey nodded and had to chuckle.

"Besides," Kate went on, checking out Zoey's outfit, "you look amazing!"

"It isn't too much?" asked Zoey.

"Are you kidding? It's just right," Kate replied. "And I really love the cardigan. Is that new? What a great touch! Oh look," she said. "We're here. Ugh, school. I can't wait for it to be summer again. Just nine more months, starting now . . ."

Before they knew it, the bus was groaning to a stop in front of their school, where a pretty blond woman was greeting students—in an adorable retro coral suit with three-quarter-length sleeves and big cloth-covered buttons on the jacket.

"Good morning." She held out a manicured hand first to Kate, then to Zoey as they walked up. Her nail polish had a touch of sparkle, Zoey noticed. "Welcome back!" she said. "I'm Ms. Austen, your new principal."

Ms. Austen? Ms. *Esther* Austen?

Wow, thought Zoey. This wasn't the old principal she expected at all!

"Hi, I'm Kate Mackey. Nice to meet you," Kate said, politely shaking hands and moving on.

"I'm Zoey. Zoey Webber," Zoey said when her turn came. "Is that suit *vintage*?"

The new principal laughed, clearly startled. "Why, yes . . . it is," she said. "My mother used to wear it in the sixties."

"I love mod," Zoey informed her. "It's my all-time favorite fashion era."

"Really? Mine too." Ms. Austen laughed and

gave Zoey's hand an extra pump. This stirred up a faint but clear scent of honeysuckle, which floated straight to Zoey's nose.

Mmm. All Zoey could think was how different this principal was from Mrs. Hammerfall, their old one, who probably hadn't smiled since around the same time as Ms. Austen's mom bought her coral suit.

"Well, it's very nice to meet you, Zoey. I think we're all going to have a great year. And I have to say, I'm happy to see that you seem excited to say good-bye to those old uniforms as well."

She cast a quick look up and down Zoey, full of approval and support, then gracefully shifted her smile to the next students walking up.

Zoey ran on to join Kate, who was waiting for her just outside the big front doors. She fiddled with her belt so it would sit just right.

"She's nice, huh?" said Kate.

"She's amazing," Zoey said. "Has there ever been a more awesome first day of school?"

As soon as she walked through the doors, however, she knew she'd spoken too soon.

The stares started immediately. The snickers right after that. The whispering . . . the pointing . . . It all came rolling in fast and furious like one of those muggy late August thunderstorms.

"What are you *wearing*?" a boy needled her as she passed him in the hall.

Zoey looked down and Kate linked her elbow.

"Just ignore him," Kate said, leading her on. "Besides, what does he know about fashion?"

Zoey tried—though what she wanted to do, really, was ask everyone the same thing. What were *they* wearing? Huh? Hadn't they gotten the letter that summer? There were no more uniforms! They didn't all have to dress alike anymore. It was cool to see that girl, Kendra, who had on a tribal-patterned dress and hot pink flats. And a guy from her math class last year had a cool skater look. But most kids were wearing the same thing: polo shirts, khakis, jeans, and tank tops. Zoey was really surprised . . . and then she remembered that standing out from the crowd was kind of scary. It made her want to crawl inside her locker to escape the stares from the other kids.

It wasn't just the students who made her self-conscious, though. Zoey hadn't even found a desk in first period social studies before the teacher was cracking a joke.

"What do we have here?" declared the bow-tied teacher, Mr. Dunn. "Halloween is in October, dear."

Zoey tried to laugh it off.

The rest of the morning, unfortunately, went pretty much the same.

In between second and third periods, she took out her phone to text Priti and Kate for moral support.

What was I thinking? she typed.

Priti replied first. **Stay strong, Zo!**

Yeah! All the Sew Zoey readers can't be wrong! Kate added.

Sure enough, when she checked the blog there were dozens of readers' comments wishing her well on her first day and saying her outfit was adorable! After that Zoey did her best to drape a thin but sturdy shrug of *I don't care* around her shoulders. Maybe, just maybe, in the future she'd tame her look a bit, she thought. But the chances of her dressing like everyone else in her school were slim to none.

Zoey knew better than to think lunch would offer her any relief from the gawks and the jeers. But she wasn't the only one, it seemed, having a rough first day.

There was a new girl. Zoey had noticed her in art class that morning. She was hard to miss. She was taller than even Kate by several inches and wore her cinnamon-colored hair in a short bob. What had most intrigued Zoey, though, was the way that she was dressed. She stood out more than anyone at Mapleton Prep in her short, lime-green overalls. Zoey had actually wanted to ask her where she got them. (They reminded Zoey of something she read in the June issue of *Très Chic* about big-name designers who also design for kids.) They weren't exactly Zoey's thing, but on the new girl they looked pretty cute.

The girl already had a tray and seemed to be looking for a seat. Zoey didn't know if she'd walked up to Ivy's table looking for one, but if she had, she'd clearly made a serious mistake.

"Look, it's the Jolly Green Giant!" said Ivy.

Bree appreciatively snorted, spraying her milk all over the place.

"Look out!" Ivy snapped, trying to dodge the spray. But she quickly refocused. "Where'd you get those overalls? Old MacDonald's farm?"

The new girl took a step back, speechless. Zoey could see her eyes fill with tears.

"What's your problem, Ivy? I mean, give her a break. She's new. Besides . . ." Zoey turned to the new girl. "Those overalls are totally cute."

"Yeah, right!" Ivy rolled her eyes, then fired them at Zoey. Zoey could tell she was trying to pick the most vulnerable place to sink her fangs. "Maybe you should worry about yourself, Zoey. What's with the *boy's* shoes?"

"*Ew!*" Zoey had wondered if Shannon would join in, and sure enough, she did. "Maybe we should call her *Joey* instead of *Zoey*," she said.

Zoey's whole body tensed. Her mouth was dry. There was a comeback somewhere inside it . . . but it wasn't coming out. What was close to coming out, though, was a hot, angry tear . . . or two, or twenty.

Zoey swallowed and gripped her tray tighter and decided it was time to move.

"Oh . . . *whatever*," she said hoarsely. Then she turned to the new girl. "C'mon. I'm *Zoey*. You can come sit with me and my friends."

---------- CHAPTER 7 ----------

Back FROM School

Well, thanks, everyone, for all your messages. I have to say they were nice to see—especially after what turned out to be a real roller coaster of a day. Yes, maybe I got a few more *What are you wearing?* looks than *You look so amazing!* compliments, and there was a certain teacher, who shall remain nameless (and whose name rhymes with Attila the Hun), who couldn't resist making a joke. And the "usual suspects" had to say something, of course, but I was expecting that.

Honestly, though, there were some high highs and some low lows. I'm glad it's over! But it also helped me realize something that I guess I always knew: I don't want to be like everyone else. I just want to be me, and if that means getting a little bit of heat in middle school, I think I can handle it.

It sure helps having my own personal cheerleading team online! I couldn't have gotten through it without you. Where did you all come from? I saw the other day that my blog traffic is up to three hundred unique visitors a day. I don't even know that many people in real life! I have two best friends, but you made me feel like I have three hundred more friends when I really needed them. Thanks!

Now I guess I have to get back on the horse. I haven't picked out my outfit for tomorrow yet, but here's a sketch of an outfit I came up with earlier today, when I was considering leaving school and moving to a desert island. Don't worry, I got over it!

Of course, Zoey didn't design a whole new outfit for every day of school. But she never went out the door in the morning without carefully thinking through everything she wore. It was like homework: What was the point of doing it if you turned it in without your name? What was the point of getting dressed, she decided, if it didn't at least kind of match who she was? The tough thing was, she wasn't exactly *sure* who she was yet, or at least what her style was. Half the fun was playing around with it and trying new looks and finding new inspiration!

And yes, there were definitely times when she wished she hadn't mixed so many plaids and checked fabrics in one outfit. Or forgotten she had gym before picking out a dress that took major maneuvering to get on and off in the locker room. But never, not once, was she sorry that she felt like her true self in her clothes. And besides, for every snarky jab she got from Ivy, Shannon, or Bree, there were comments from other kids that were complimentary.

"Did you make that shoelace necklace? Cool!"

"I love your bubble skirt! Where'd you get it?"

Not to mention the undeniable nod of approval that the principal, Ms. Austen, greeted Zoey with every morning. It was like an immunity booster that helped power her through the day.

Her blog was getting more followers also. A hundred new ones in a week! Where did they come from? Zoey wondered. She didn't think it was kids from school. She hadn't told a soul—except Libby, the new girl, who turned out to be as nice as she was shy. And Zoey had made it very clear to Kate and Priti that for now, at least, she liked keeping a wide moat between her real life and her cyber one.

She tried to update her blog every day with a new look and at least a line or two of thoughts, but sometimes it was hard to fit it in. She seemed to have twice as much homework this year as last year—maybe even more. And then there were Kate and Priti, who were 100 percent behind her blog, of course. But they were also 100 percent behind "don't forget about your friends!" and "hang out with us!"

"You'll be at my soccer game tonight, right?"

asked Kate as soon as the season began.

And so Zoey stayed after school with Priti and went to Kate's first home game.

That day she'd worn a white cotton sundress with green flats that she'd drawn zigzags on in permanent marker and a short-sleeved bolero jacket that she'd made out of her dad's old sport coat. It was a brownish, orangish, greenish herringbone fabric that she'd never thought much of. But now, cut down and trimmed with brown velvet ribbon, it was positively beauteous!

There were no bleachers around the field, just grass, so Zoey and Priti stood. They waved to Kate, and she waved back as she huddled with her team around their coach. They were playing St. Bernadette's, unfortunately, who were known for their swift and sure defeats. Zoey was not looking forward to Kate's mood after the game, and she hoped she scored a goal, at least.

She also hoped the freshly cut grass wouldn't stain her dress. *White? What was I thinking?* she wondered as she looked at the juicy green blades.

"Do you want to sit down?" asked Priti.

"Uh-uh!" said Zoey. "No way."

"Hey, look. Here comes Ms. Austen," Priti said, nodding down the field.

Zoey turned to see the principal gliding toward them across the lawn in three-inch heels.

Let St. B.'s have the best sports teams. We have her! Zoey thought. Was she actually feeling Mapleton Prep school pride?

Zoey had to admit that she'd never tried to imagine the perfect principal. (Had anyone even paired those two words together before?) But if she had to now, Zoey knew what she would do: She'd start with Ms. Austen—and she'd stop there too.

Ms. Austen was just really calm and cheerful and . . . reliable . . . like a TV talent show's "nice" judge. Zoey bet there was nothing she wouldn't do for a student, no matter how weird or *unconventional* that student was. And if, knock on wood, the whole school suddenly went up in flames, Zoey could see her pulling every student out of the fire—in designer heels, if she had to.

And speaking of heels, Zoey had already noticed in just a few weeks a wonderful pattern in the principal's dress. Mondays and Wednesdays were suits. They could be pantsuits or skirts. And it had not been lost on Zoey the clever way she accessorized them. Tuesdays and Thursdays were dresses—sometimes a shirtdress or a wrap dress, but usually sheaths. And Fridays could be anything, just so it was black—and could go from day to evening (or so Zoey guessed since she had read about day-to-night outfits in magazines). In fact, Zoey had spent many a Friday morning, while Mr. Dunn droned on and on, imagining exactly how Ms. Austen might later pull off the transformation. A necklace, perhaps, and some earrings that dangled and sparkled (but not too much). Maybe she'd swap her plain heels for some strappier sandals. . . .

Today was a Thursday, and she was wearing a cobalt A-line dress with a color-block pattern.

"Hi, girls," the principal said with a smile that made her eyes squint, so Zoey knew it was real.

"Hi, Ms. Austen," said Zoey and Priti, almost together. They looked at each other and grinned.

"How nice of you two to come out to support

the team. How can they lose, right, with you here to cheer for them?"

Priti squeezed some air into her cheeks and tried not to laugh.

Zoey shrugged and gently explained, "We're really just here for our friend, Kate. I hate to break it to you, but our team doesn't stand a chance."

"No?" Ms. Austen looked out onto the field, where the game had just begun. "Oh . . . hmm . . . yes . . . St. Bernadette's does look pretty tough." She sighed and turned back to the girls, smiling. "That's a lovely jacket, Zoey. I've never seen one quite like it before. Is it . . . vintage?" she asked.

Zoey adjusted the lapels. "Kind of . . ."

"She *made* it," Priti said proudly.

Ms. Austen crossed her arms. "Really? I am impressed!"

"Well, I made it . . . but I didn't *make* it make it," Zoey quickly clarified. "I started with one of my dad's old sport coats. There were some moth holes down at the bottom and the elbows were worn out. . . ." Zoey grinned. "And if I didn't do something with it, he was going to wear it again."

Ms. Austen laughed. "So you reused the fabric?"

Zoey nodded. "Yes, exactly. Basically."

"Well, you know . . . ," said Ms. Austen as her smile began to change. Somewhere behind her smoky blue eyes, wheels began to spin. "We're having a fund-raiser coming up. Have you heard about it? A fashion show and auction . . ."

Zoey nodded. "Sure. For the music department, right?" She'd seen a sign in the lobby—and something on the school website.

"Exactly," said Ms. Austen. "I'm hoping to use it to kick-start a bigger program. Maybe even a marching band. We did something like it at my last school, and it was a great success. We're getting some dress stores downtown to donate outfits, and the students will model them—and hopefully lots of parents will bid and take them home at the end."

"It sounds great," said Zoey. She looked at Priti, who was nodding. "We'll definitely go."

"Well, *I* was thinking, how would you like to help out?" Ms. Austen asked.

Help? Her? Huh?

"Um . . . I don't know," Zoey said. She smiled

back at Ms. Austen, but she couldn't help shaking her head. The thought of walking down a runway in front of a room full of Mapleton parents gave her an instant stomachache. She could see Ms. Austen's puzzled reaction, and she tried her best to explain. "I'm sorry, Ms. Austen, but even if it is for a really good cause . . . I don't know if I could."

"I'll do it, though!" said Priti. "I mean, I've never modeled before, but I'll try."

"That's great!" Ms. Austen smiled at her. "You'll be wonderful, I know. But actually . . ." She turned back to Zoey. "I had a slightly different idea."

A different idea? thought Zoey. *Wait a second. Even if I don't want to model in the show, she should still give me a chance to do it! That's not like her at all.*

So what was it Ms. Austen wanted her to do? Sell tickets? DJ? Zoey tried not to look too disappointed while she waited for Ms. Austen to go on.

"How would you like . . . I mean, I know this is a lot to ask. . . ." Ms. Austen slipped a glossy nail between her lips and bit down on the tip. "I was just thinking how nice it would be, Zoey, if you could design and donate a dress for the auction."

Zoey scoured Ms. Austen's face for signs that she was joking, but the principal's expression was nothing but totally serious.

"Are you kidding?! Of course she would!" said Priti before Zoey could say a word.

"Oh, I think Zoey better answer this herself," Ms. Austen said. "It would be a lot of work."

Yes, thought Zoey. It *would* be a lot of work. It was sure to take a lot of time. . . . But to design and make a dress for a real, live fashion show? How could she pass up a chance like that?

"Oh, I'd love to do it, Ms. Austen!" she said. "Thank you! Thank you so much! I will not let you down, I promise."

"*Yay!*" All of a sudden, ecstatic cheers rang out.

Zoey spun around. What was that? Was the whole sideline cheering for her? Zoey was confused. . . .

"Hey, look!" said Priti, pointing. She started jumping up and down. "Kate scored a goal!"

"Yay, Kate!" Zoey shouted automatically as she started to jump too.

Yay, Kate! And yay, me! she thought. *And yay, fashion show!*

-------- CHAPTER 8 --------

Mapleton Fashion Show Ideas

Muchas, muchas gracias, mis amigos, (does that count as Spanish homework, do you think?) for all your comments on my designs the other day. Those of you who said dress B was too Lady Gaga, yes, you were absolutely right. I totally see it now. And I was wondering who'd catch the obvious influence of Daphne Shaw in dress A. I'm sorry. Sometimes I can't help it. Her clothes are so amazing!

The big news is . . . drumroll, please . . . that the school principal asked me to design a dress for my school's fashion show fund-raiser! I'm going to be designing a real dress for a real fashion show! Really! I know, right? It's for the music department, and I'm the only student designer, and I can't believe she wants me to do it! And this is the outfit I was wearing on the fateful day that she asked me: The white sundress was my mom's. I had to cinch the back together with a binder clip to make it fit right, but with the jacket on top no one could tell. Oh. Oops! I guess my secret's out. Oh well! ☺ And I made that little bolero jacket out of my dad's old blazer. It was looking kind of frumpy before, but now it has a fabulous new life, right? And Ms. Austen LOVED it. And last but not least, see the green flats? I drew those squiggles in the middle of study hall. . . . (After I had finished my homework, I promise!) I'd say it was an excellent use of my time, don't you think?

Well, I guess it's back to the drawing board, then, literally. . . . I don't have much time to design and sew this fashion show outfit, whatever it ends up being. I'm going to head to the thrift store to see if I can find some inspiration. I have a whole new appreciation now for what real designers must go through when they're on a deadline! I feel so (kind of, maybe, a little) grown-up!

"So . . . what are we looking for exactly here?" Kate asked as she flipped through a flimsy chrome rack with the sign WOMEN'S DRESSES taped to the side.

Zoey looked over her shoulder and shrugged. "I'm not sure," she replied. She turned back to the rack labeled WOMEN'S LONG-SLEEVE TOPS. "When I see it, I'll know . . . I hope."

They were at the thrift store, along with Priti, on a mission to find *something*—even if they didn't know what. Something to help Zoey come up with an amazing design for the two-weeks-away Mapleton Prep fashion show. Yes, Zoey knew she had plenty of sketches she could just go with (which was what Kate and Priti had urged her to do several times), but she also knew that actually constructing any of them with her current sewing skills would be a challenge. She had no idea how to make her own patterns, and though it was something she wanted to learn, she didn't quite see it happening in time for the show. She decided to do some kind of a twist on a classic shape.

Kate held up a bright pink muumuu wide enough to shroud her mom's minivan. "How about this?" she called to Zoey. "Does *this* give you any ideas?"

Zoey winced. "Oh yeah. But you don't want to know them. *Please* put that thing back." She laughed.

"I don't know . . . ," Kate went on. "I think we should *all* try it on. Together! Hey, Priti." She looked around. "Where'd she go?"

Zoey nodded toward the back, past the shoes, to the toys and games and books. "Guess."

"Oh right." Kate laughed. "Fifty-cent paper-backs. Of course."

Zoey moved away from the shirts and joined Kate by the dress rack. She pulled out a denim dress and considered it. What was she thinking? She put it back.

"How ugly is this?" said Kate, holding up the

lace-edged sleeve of a purple-rose-covered print.

"Uh, Kate . . ." Zoey grinned. "I'm pretty sure your mom has that dress in yellow."

Kate eyed it again. "Oh my gosh, you're right! She totally does. Oops!" She giggled and shoved it back into its place. "Don't tell her I said that, okay? I don't want to hurt her feelings."

"Of course not. Hey, let's look over there," Zoey said, pointing to the end of the row, where a single, lonely, "formal wear" rack held a few dangling dresses.

Zoey had been to the thrift store enough times to be able to guess where the dresses were from. Pastels came from bridesmaids—pretty much as soon as the wedding cake was cut. Jewel colors came from high school seniors the day after their prom.

For a change, though, there was something different on the rack this time—something you didn't see every day: an almost shiny, meringue-like wedding dress with ginormous, ruffled sleeves.

"Do you think someone actually wore this?" Kate asked, pushing its rustley neighbors aside.

"Oh, I'm sure they did," said Zoey. "That's the thing about fashion, you know? In the 1980s, this was *it*. Remember *Sixteen Candles*?" She checked the price tag. "Twenty dollars. You know, it's probably worth that just for all this lace . . . if it wasn't so yellow." Unfortunately, it also kind of reminded her of a doily.

"Let's check out the skirts." Zoey grabbed Kate's hand and started to pull her down the aisle. Then all of a sudden they heard the *"Du-du-dahhhh, du-du-dahhhh, du-du-dahhhh"* of the "Stars and Stripes Forever."

Zoey spun around. "What is *that*?"

They both stopped and looked around until they spotted the source. It was Priti marching toward them with a lanky brass trombone, wearing a deep blue-and-yellow marching-band coat.

"What do you think?" She stopped humming and whipped her shoulders and her horn to the right and the left. As she did, Zoey caught the design on the back: a big, grinning bumblebee.

"Is it *me*?" Priti asked. "I'm thinking yes. Maybe I should join the new marching band!"

Whoa. Zoey wasn't sure if it was just a feeling . . . or if a light bulb really had just gone off in her head. "Where did you *find* that, Priti?"

"With the toys and books and stuff," Priti said.

"It's amazing!"

"You think?" said Priti. She held the trombone out for Zoey to take.

"Not that!" Zoey told her. "The coat. The *coat!* It's perfect!"

She reached out and traced her index finger along the gold braid that loop-de-looped along the sleeves. It curled all the way up to the shoulders, where stiff gold epaulettes rained gold fringe down over it. There were more ropes of gold crisscrossing the front, and three rows of shiny, nickel-size brass buttons.

"Really?" said Kate. She looked worried. "I don't know, Zo. . . . It's cool, but I don't think this is what Ms. Austen has in mind . . . at all."

"Yeah." Priti nodded. "Remember, Zo. You want to make something that people will want to bid on in the auction. Don't you?"

"Relax, guys," said Zoey. "I don't mean I want

to use this actual coat." At least, she thought, not for the fashion show . . . "But all this braid and fringe and buttons . . . They're classic trimmings for marching-band uniforms. The fashion show is raising money for the music department, so it's perfect!"

Priti turned her back so it faced Zoey. "And don't forget the bee!"

"Funny." Zoey grinned and turned to Kate. "So we're good. Now all we have to do is go back home and measure you. "

"Measure me?" Kate pulled her chin in. "What are you talking about? Why?"

"So we know the dress that I make will fit you," said Zoey. "It's going to be kind of sporty, and I think it would look great on you!"

"Make it fit *me*?" Kate took a step back, as if she were about to run for her life.

"Watch out!" Zoey warned as Kate nearly knocked down a rack of purses. "Anyway, just think about it, okay?" she asked.

Kate's head began to shake. "Wait. You're joking, right?"

"No, not really," said Zoey. "It would be a big help!"

"I'm helping by being here with you. And I'll go to the show . . . to *watch* and cheer you on. But I'm not walking down a runway or anything. No way. Sorry, Zo."

Zoey sighed. "Okay, then . . . Priti, you're hired." She turned to her friend. Priti would walk down anything, no problem. So why wasn't she smiling back?

"But . . . I already have a dress, Zo. . . . I picked it out and it's all set," Priti said. "I don't know if I can change it now. Why don't *you* just model it?"

"Yeah." Kate nodded. "You should do it. After all, it's your dress."

"Exactly!" said Zoey. "Which is why I can't do it. Designers don't model their own clothes."

"I'm sure some of them do," Kate told her.

"But it's easier to do dress fittings on someone else." Zoey crossed her arms. "Come on, Kate. *Please.*" Zoey pleaded. "Just this once? You might even have fun!"

Kate crossed her arms right back at Zoey and

flatly shook her head. Zoey got it, of course, since she didn't want to be up there onstage any more than Kate.

"You should do it, Zo," said Priti.

"But, guys, I'm going to be nervous enough just showing a dress—I know it. There's no way I can *model* it in front of everyone, too."

"Well, then," Kate said simply, "ask somebody else. Sorry, Zoey."

Zoey sighed. "It's okay. I'm sorry too."

She tried to quickly think of who she could ask to model now that Kate was out. She bet the girls who'd be most interested had, like Priti, already answered the call. But the more she pondered the word "model," the more one image came to her mind: tall, willowy Libby. The new girl!

Oh my gosh! thought Zoey. How great would *Libby* look in Zoey's clothes!

Zoey decided to ask Libby the big question at lunch on Monday. She waited until they were all seated at the table that Libby had begun to share with her, Priti, and Kate. Little by little, Libby had opened up to them, and they'd learned a lot in the past few weeks. Her family had moved to town for her dad's work as a scientist at a research lab. Her mom was an emergency room nurse at the local hospital. She had a sister in kindergarten who was also the tallest girl in her class. And her green overalls were, in fact, designer, though she hadn't realized it until Zoey asked. She said her aunt lived in New York and was always sending her stuff like that. She definitely wasn't in the Kate or Priti category of best-friends-for-life yet, but she'd become a good new friend.

Zoey watched as Libby dipped her first french fry into her ketchup, then she took a deep breath and opened her mouth.

"So, Libby . . . I have a question. . . ."

"Uh-huh?" Libby nibbled her fry.

"I was just wondering. . . ." Zoey paused.

Priti gave her the *get on with it* wave.

"This fashion show coming up . . . ," Zoey continued.

"Yeah?"

"Well, have you signed up for it or anything?"

Libby's head swung back and forth. "No. I feel

like I'm still getting used to this place. I don't think I'm ready for stuff like that yet."

"Oh!" Zoey leaned forward. Talk about perfect openings! "But that's why it would be such a great thing for you to do!" She nodded to Kate and Priti. "Right, guys? Don't you think?"

"Yeah, totally!" said Priti.

"Oh my gosh, yes!" Kate agreed.

Libby shrugged. "Well . . . maybe the next thing. I'm sure it's too late to sign up now." She grinned at Zoey and Priti and Kate and gulped down another fry. "What?" She wiped the corners of her mouth. "What are you all staring at? Do I have ketchup on my face?"

"Actually," said Zoey, "it's not too late. It's not too late at all. I still need someone to model *my* dress."

"*Your* dress?" Libby swallowed.

Oh, please don't say no, Zoey begged in her mind.

She nodded. "Uh-huh. I just decided this weekend what I'm going to do, and it's going to be really cool. And I really, really think, Libby, that it would look awesome on you. Please say yes!"

"It should be a lot of fun," said Priti. "And you know I'll be there doing it too."

"Yeah," Kate said. "And I'll be watching . . . and it would take a *lot* of pressure off me."

Libby opened her mouth. Then closed it. Then opened it again. "Well . . . if you really want me to . . . *Yes!* Thanks! I totally will!"

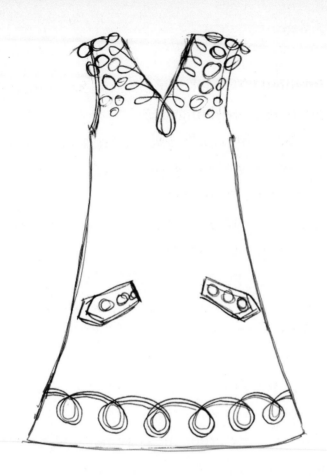

------- CHAPTER 9 -------

Band Coat . . . Deconstructed!

What do you think of the final design for the fashion show? I'm pretty happy with it and have to thank Fashionsista for her comment about what to do with the epaulettes. Pockets! Of course! What would I do without you? They're perfect, right?

And the next thank-you goes out to my aunt. She surprised me this weekend with an out-of-the-blue "just because I love you" gift. A real dress form! I can adjust the measurements and everything! And I've decided to name her after the only other headless beauty I know of . . . Ladies and gentlemen, my new muse is called Marie Antoinette, s'il vous plaît!

So that's all for tonight. Signing off early so I can get back to work. It's going to be a long night. . . .

Finally, it was done!

Or was it . . . ?

That was the problem, Zoey realized, with finishing something before it was due: You always had more time to keep working on it. But Zoey didn't *really* have more time. There was something else she had due on Friday, in addition to the dress for the fashion show: her first big social studies paper for Mr. Dunn—which she still had to start. Well, she had a subject at least. Athena, the goddess of war, or wisdom, or something. But she still had to write the five-page report—plus bibliography.

"Hey, honey." Zoey's dad appeared in the dining room doorway. He leaned against the frame. "I was afraid you were still up. Lights-out, Zo. It's after eleven, and you're never going to get up for school in the morning if you don't go to bed."

"I will," she assured him. She yawned. "I just want to get this dress finished first. What do you think?" She spun Marie around so her dad could see the front.

Jan had helped her pick out a classic sheath dress pattern and given her some tips for "spicing it up," while Zoey found a rich cherry fabric that screamed "bandleader" to her. The dress pattern looked simple . . . but the look was deceiving, Zoey found, when she actually started to sew. It was her first zipper ever, not to mention her first up-close-and-personal encounter with darts, folds sewn into fabric to give it more shape. She ended up taking it back to the store three times for Jan's tech support. All she could think about was how glad she was there weren't any sleeves to worry about. The most time-consuming part of it all, however, was laying out all the braid and buttons and sewing them all on. Zoey had tried a dozen designs at least before finally deciding.

"Wow," her dad said. "It looks great to me. What else in the world would you do?"

Zoey shrugged. "I don't know . . . Maybe add some more braid . . . here . . . and here. . . . Maybe take some off here . . . and here . . . and fix the little ripple in the hem."

"Oh, *Zo*." Her dad rolled his eyes fondly. "You're just like your mom in so many ways."

Zoey smiled. She loved it when he told her little things like that about her mom.

"And you know what I always told her?"

"No, what?" she eagerly asked.

"Sometimes you just have to take a step *back* and know when it's time to say when."

Zoey leaned back on her hands. "And did she listen to you, Dad?"

He rubbed the day's worth of beard on his chin, which was grayer than his hair. "Not always, no . . . but that's not my point," he said with a sleepy grin. "My point," he went on, "is that you've been holed up in here now all weekend and most of the week before. If you ask me, the dress you made looks perfect and tomorrow's Monday and you need to get some sleep."

Zoey sighed and nodded slowly. He was probably right. Plus, she had to remember what she'd said in her blog herself more than once: The only thing worse than an unfinished look was a look that was overdone.

"You know what I'm going to do," she said. "I'm going to take it in to school tomorrow and leave it with the other clothes for the show, and if I *really* want to work on it any more, I'll just work on it there."

"Great idea!" her dad told her. "Good night?"

"Mmm-hmm. Good night, Dad," said Zoey. "And thanks a lot. I'm just going to move these two buttons here . . . and then I'll go right up."

"Yep, you're just like your mom," he said as he headed for the stairs.

The next morning, Zoey zipped the dress up in a long, black garment bag and carefully toted it to school.

"Ooh! Let me see it!" Kate begged as soon as she climbed on the bus.

"Not here," said Zoey. "At school. I don't want to risk messing it up. I posted a sketch of it on my blog last night. Did you check it out?"

Kate shook her head and stuck her lip out in a pout. "I was doing math homework and somehow I just forgot."

Math homework? Oh no . . .

"I totally forgot about the math homework," said Zoey. "Do you think I can get it done at lunch?"

"Probably." Kate nodded. "Well, how 'bout the Spanish? Did you do that?"

"Oh boy. I'm in trouble." She moaned.

All she could think, looking down at the dress in her lap, was that it was a good thing it was out of her dining room. She could only imagine all the homework she'd never get done this week if she'd kept it at home.

When they got to school, Zoey headed straight for the auditorium, with Kate by her side. Then they ran into Ivy just outside the backstage door.

"What's in the bag?" Ivy asked.

Zoey came *this* close to answering with "none of your beeswax," but she bit her tongue. "Oh, it's my dress for the fashion show."

"Yeah." Kate nodded next to her. "The one that *she* designed and made herself."

Zoey watched as Ivy's face turned from smug to puzzled and to at last envious.

"You made it?" Ivy choked, as if the words had stung her throat.

"Uh-huh." Zoey nodded.

Kate knocked open the stage door with her hip. "Come on, Zo. We'd better hurry or we're going to be late for first period."

"Wait," blurted Ivy. "Can I see it?"

"Sure," Zoey said, following Kate. "On Friday. Like everyone else. It's going to be a big reveal."

That was *sort* of true, but Zoey also didn't want to give Ivy the chance to say something mean, as usual. Why else would she want to see it?

"Did you see her face?" Zoey asked.

"I know! That was awesome!" Kate laughed. "So . . . where are you going to put this?" she asked, looking around the cluttered space.

"I was hoping there was a hook . . . ," said Zoey. And sure enough, there was—right under a shelf, to the side of the curtain control panel.

Zoey hung up the garment bag, feeling extremely satisfied.

"This'll be great," she said. "It'll be right here, all ready for the show."

"Well, can I see it already?" Kate asked her.

Zoey grinned and unzipped the bag. "Ta-da!" she said dramatically, stepping back.

"Oh my gosh, Zo! It's amazing!" cried Kate.

Zoey exhaled with delight and relief.

BRRINNNNGG.

Zoey and Kate looked at each other, knowing that the bell meant they had better go.

Quickly, Zoey zipped the vinyl garment bag back up and gave the shoulders a tender pat. "I'll be back to check on you after school."

And with that she grabbed Kate's hand and they hurried off to their first class.

"Libby, wait till you see Zoey's dress!" Kate said at lunch as soon as she set down her tray. "You too."

She turned to Priti. "You're going to love it!"

"It's finished! Oh, I can't wait," said Libby. "When can I try it on, do you think?"

"What? Is it here?" Priti asked.

Zoey nodded. "My dad said I was spending way too much time on it . . . and I kind of guess maybe I was, so I decided to bring it in and hang it up backstage—and hopefully start getting some homework done."

"Do you think we have time to go now?" Priti shot an eager look at the cafeteria clock.

Zoey shook her head and pointed to the thick book in front of her. "I really have to get this math done now—or as much of it as I can. How about after school? You all can stay for a little while, can't you? We'll take the late bus."

They met in the hall by Zoey's locker after eighth period and went to the auditorium from there.

The bag was hanging right where Zoey left it, but there wasn't much room, so she let Priti, Kate, and Libby run up to it first. She knew they'd say something nice no matter what, and yet she was still nervous. She hung back and waited . . . and waited some more. But they didn't say *anything*. Did they hate it that much? Her heart sank to the deep, dark bottom of her gut. She really thought they would love it!

But then she looked at their faces when they came back, and her doubt changed to fear. They looked like they'd seen a ghost.

"What's wrong?" She started toward them, and Kate held up her hand to stop her.

"You left the bag zipped up, didn't you?" Kate asked.

Zoey nodded. "Uh-huh. Why? Was it unzipped when you got here?"

Kate nodded slowly.

Priti sucked her lip.

Libby's eyes seemed to get red.

"What?" Zoey couldn't take it any longer. She ran up to see for herself. And that's when she saw the bag splayed open, revealing her once red, now yellow-paint-covered dress.

A can of paint lay on the shelf above it, empty and on its side. Only then did Zoey notice how the entire shelf was jam-packed with old paint cans.

"I'm so sorry . . . ," Libby murmured.

"Can we fix it?" Priti asked.

Zoey tried, but there was no way to make her mouth answer no. All she could do was sink to the rough, dusty floor.

CHAPTER 10

Band Coat . . . Destroyed

So remember that dress I posted yesterday? Of course you do. How could you not? Well, I'm glad that you remember it because now it's ruined. Covered in paint. Completely and utterly destroyed. And I don't exactly know what happened either. Every time I think about it—like right now—I'm literally blinded by these stupid tears of mine. Besides, I should really be writing the social studies paper that's due Friday instead of feeling sorry for myself. Oh well . . . Maybe I jumped into this fashion show thing too quickly. What would a real designer do if their clothes were ruined? All I can say is I definitely learned a lesson today . . . even if I'm not sure that I know what it is.

As my dad likes to say: "When life gives you lemons, make lemon meringue pie." (That's not a typo. He likes pie more than lemonade.) Maybe paint splatters will be the next big thing in fashion? What do you think? Hey, I tried. ☺

"I think Ivy did it," Kate said. Her big Bambi eyes narrowed into slits.

Priti's jaw clenched in agreement. "Are you kidding? Of course she did."

It was Tuesday morning, and Ivy had just walked down the hall. Zoey hadn't missed her sideways glances—or her uncomfortably bent head. Zoey slammed her locker shut and stared bitterly away.

So what if she did? Zoey couldn't prove it . . . and it sure didn't change the fact that she had no dress for Friday night.

Her friends had already urged her to make another one. But they didn't understand. She'd spent something like fifty hours, at *least*, on that dress, and there was no way on earth she could do that again. Especially when she still had that stupid social studies paper to write! Plus, even if she made the basic shape of the dress, she didn't have the trimmings from the uniform.

"Maybe you can try asking Mr. Dunn for an extension . . . ?" suggested Libby.

"Yeah!" said Kate. "You totally should."

"But he already said no extensions," said Zoey. "And not just once—like, twenty times."

"These are extenuating circumstances!" said Priti. "What do you have to lose?"

As it turned out . . . nothing really, except five minutes of her life.

The moment she asked the question, she knew she'd wasted her breath. Mr. Dunn stared down his nose at her calmly and jabbed his thumb over his shoulder at the board. "What does it say?"

Zoey knew he wasn't talking about the date or their assignment. (Still, she was tempted to say exactly that.) He was talking about the large block letters along the whole bottom.

Zoey squeezed her fingers and cleared her throat. "'No extensions,'" she read.

"And there's your answer," he told her.

"But . . ."

"There are no 'buts' in social studies," he said soberly. "Now, please take your seat, won't you?"

Zoey spent the rest of first period—and second also—swinging between moods. On one side was anger, on the other impending gloom.

When the bell for third period finally rang, she started for art class, then turned around. She had to talk to Ms. Austen. It was her only hope.

"Hello there. May I help you?" Mrs. Beckstein, the secretary, looked up from her desk of forty-five years. "Do you need to see the nurse?" she asked. "You're looking very pale."

Zoey shook her head. "No, ma'am. I wanted to see Ms. Austen. Is she, um, around?"

Mrs. Beckstein placed her shaky palms on the sides of the blotter in front of her. "Well . . . yes, I believe so. Give me just a second. Tell me, what's your name, sweetheart?"

"Zoey. Zoey Webber. It's about the fashion show," she said.

Mrs. Beckstein pushed herself up and made her way across the office on fat cream-colored shoes. Her lavender dress, Zoey noticed, was just a shade darker than her hair. *Hmm* . . . When Zoey's hair went gray in the far, far future, that was a look she might just try, she thought. Or maybe she'd match her hair to the magenta tunic she made a few weeks ago. She could just imagine Dad's face if she came home with magenta hair! Just thinking about it made her smile a little.

When the secretary came to the door labeled PRINCIPAL, she rapped politely beneath the sign. She looked back and smiled at Zoey, then turned the knob and stepped inside.

"Come right in." She emerged and waved her fingers as a signal for Zoey to approach.

Zoey obeyed and was suddenly aware of how

very heavy her legs felt. It was like walking through a swimming pool . . . or maybe quicksand.

Mrs. Beckstein shut the door gently behind Zoey, leaving Zoey to gaze around. The principal's office looked much different than it had when Zoey presented her petition to Mrs. Hammerfall the year before. She distinctly remembered not being able to breathe and counting the seconds until Mrs. H. let her leave.

Since then, Ms. Austen had somehow transformed the starched room into a . . . cozy space. The walls were no longer beige, but a warm apple green. They were dressed with crystal-clear photographs of lily ponds and fuzzy paintings of the beach. And nowhere did Zoey see a single framed diploma or Latin degree. It was more like a home than an office. Plants lined the sunny windowsill and propped-up books on the shelves. A vase full of enormous orange roses took up a whole corner of her sleek, polished desk.

Ms. Austen smiled and stood up, then offered her hand. "Hi, Zoey! So what brings you here instead of to third period?" she cheerfully asked.

Zoey's throat went dry. The whole thing was so disappointing, and having to talk about it out loud made it feel more real.

"I . . . I just wanted to tell you that I'm really sorry. . . ." She gulped. "But I'm not going to have a dress after all for the fashion show on Friday night."

"What?" gasped Ms. Austen, looking sincerely upset. "Please." She gestured to the plush chair next to Zoey. "Sit down and tell me what happened. I don't understand. . . ."

Zoey sat. She breathed in the roses. Or was it the principal's perfume? Whatever it was, it was nice. She inhaled again, hoping it would steady her. It did a little, but not enough.

"I . . . I made it. . . . And then yesterday I brought it into school . . . and, well, I thought if I left it in the auditorium, it would be safe until Friday, but . . . I was wrong."

"Why? What happened?"

"I . . . I don't really know. There were these paint cans, I guess, on a shelf above it, and . . . somehow . . . one of them fell down."

"Oh no!" Ms. Austen leaned in. "And it's ruined?"

"Pretty much."

"I am so very sorry," said Ms. Austen. She truly looked as if she were. "And there's no way you can make another now by Friday, I suppose."

Zoey shook her head. "No. I don't see how. You see . . . I have this social studies paper to do for Mr. Dunn by Friday too."

"Ah, I see." Ms. Austen nodded slowly

"The thing is . . . I asked him for an extension."

"Yes?" said Ms. Austen. "And what did he say?"

Zoey took a deep breath. "No . . . but he wouldn't let me explain!" She sat up on her hands and leaned toward Ms. Austen. Her heart was racing now. "But if you told him, Ms. Austen, he'd have to listen and change his mind."

The principal sat back. "And how long have you had this assignment?" she asked.

Zoey considered the question. "Two . . . two and a half weeks."

Ms. Austen rubbed her chin slowly, and Zoey knew her answer before it came out.

"Well, Zoey, you had every right to ask for an extension, but I have to respect Mr. Dunn's answer as well. This is, after all, a school, and as such, schoolwork must come first. I wish there was something I could do, but I'm afraid this is all up to you. It would be *such* a shame, but if you can't create a dress *and* finish your paper, then we'll just have to wait till next year to have one of your designs in the fashion show."

Zoey nodded.

"But," she went on, "this doesn't mean you have to miss being in the show altogether. It's not the same thing at all, I know, but you could still model a dress. It's only Tuesday, so there's still plenty of time for you to pick one out to wear Friday night."

Zoey shrugged. She knew Ms. Austen meant well, but being at the show without her dress would only make her feel even worse. "Thanks, Ms. Austen. But I don't think I could."

"I understand," said Ms. Austen. "I'm sorry, Zoey. I really am."

She rose from her chair, and Zoey did too.

"By the way, what's your paper on?" she asked as she walked to the door.

Zoey heaved the name "Athena" out along.

"The goddess of weaving. How perfect for you."

Weaving?

"I thought she was the goddess of war and stuff like that."

"Ah." Ms. Austen's smile was wise and also warm. "Keep doing your research."

CHAPTER 11

Thank You Sew Much!

Wow! Where did you all come from? Heaven or what? What can I say but thank you all for telling me not to give up on this dress! I'm following your advice and taking a shot at doing a simpler version. You're right, I'm probably the only one who will notice what's missing or different. And no, I couldn't get an extension on the social studies paper (I know!), but that's actually okay. Mr. Dunn's probably right, and besides, I've learned a lot about Athena. Did you know that she was the goddess of weaving and arts and crafts and not just of war and wisdom? I did a little drawing inspired by her while I was waiting for Dad at the gas station (since that was the only second I had that wasn't spent sewing or writing). Notice the draping of the fabric . . . very ancient-Greek-inspired chic!

And now, back to the modern (but not at all Greek) tragedy of my dress for the fashion show: I can't tell you what I'll be able to make now, with so little time. But all I can do is my best, right? And yes, music fans and ex–band geeks (your words, not mine) . . . you're all 100 percent right. It is for a good cause! And just as soon as I have something to show you, you'll be the first to know. TTYS!

"Dad? Are you ready? I think we'd better go."

"Almost!" Zoey's dad called down from upstairs. "Just looking for that tie you like."

Zoey sighed and returned to pacing across the front hall rug. She wasn't sure if it was nerves that were making her so jumpy or exhaustion from being up late the night before. She paused by the mirror and gauged her outfit one more time—at least what she could see of it from the waist up. She'd decided on black (since it was, after all, what Daphne Shaw always wore at her shows) and gone with black jeans after sewing a row of black beaded ribbon down each side, tuxedo-pants style. She paired them with an oversize silver shirt from her mom's closet (for good luck). Well, on her mom it was probably a regular shirt, but on Zoey it was more like a tunic, and she had to layer another shirt underneath. Her favorite part, though, was the vest, which she made out of the black remnants Jan gave her the first time she went to the fabric store. The front was solid, and the back had a zigzag pattern on one side, and black-and-white check on the other.

"Dad." She groaned. This was torture. She had to get to school! Libby hadn't even tried on the second dress she'd made yet . . . since Zoey had just finished

it that Friday afternoon. It was sure to need some last-minute tweaking, and who knew how long that would take?

Right now, while she was waiting, the dress hung on the back of the coat closet door. She'd tried her best to give it the same feel of the first dress. She'd managed to salvage most of the buttons and gotten more gold braid—though it was much thinner—at A Stitch in Time.

When she walked into the store, she headed straight to Jan, who was standing at the counter. She began to tell Jan about the ruined dress, but Jan stopped her before she was done.

"Wait! Zoey! I know the whole story! I heard about the Sew Zoey blog at my quilting circle last week, so I started reading it a few days ago and caught up on the blog posts. I didn't realize Sew Zoey was *you* until I saw the sketch of your dress. I was hoping you'd come back here so I could tell you in person how much I love your blog!" She walked around the counter and gave Zoey a big hug.

"Really? You read Sew Zoey?" asked Zoey.

"Yes, I do. And that's how I know you're in a

pinch. I want to help, if I can. You know, we've all had these things happen to us. A few years ago we had a crazy hurricane come through and my whole shop flooded. The insurance didn't cover half the damage, I'll tell you that right now."

"So what'd you do?" asked Zoey.

"What'd I do? I'll tell you what I did. I decided right then and there that I was done with this retail stuff. It was a sign that it was time to retire, I thought . . . and then my customers started to call. 'When are you reopening?' they'd ask me. 'We can't live without you!' they'd go on. And when I told them I was closing up shop, do you know what they did? They offered to help. They came in here and cleaned for me and went around collecting donations to rebuild my stock."

"Really?" said Zoey.

Jan put her hand on her hip. "Why in the world would I lie to you? In fact, that's just why I'm going to help *you*, little lady. Paying it forward, as they say. Everything you need to make a new dress, it's on the house!" Jan declared.

"Thank you so much, Jan!" Zoey exclaimed.

Of course, Zoey didn't have time to sew a new dress as complicated as the first one, but Jan had a solution for this problem too. "Go simple," she said. "And go with something you know like the back of your hand. I'm thinking of the first things you made this summer. Those dear little beach cover-ups. Remember those?"

"Yes . . . ," Zoey said, rather halfheartedly. "But that's kind of . . . beachy . . . don't you think?"

Jan looked at her over her glasses, down her nose. "Well, if you make it out of white terry cloth, yes, certainly. But out of that gorgeous red fabric you picked out last time? Absolutely not! And if I remember correctly, that pattern was one size fits all, yes? No measuring. No fuss. You won't even have to take time cutting out a *new* pattern. Just use the one you have and voilà!"

"Oh right!" Zoey said as the light bulb went on over her own head.

Jan was totally right, of course! She made a new dress that looked a lot like the original one. And today was the big day, and she was ready to go, dress in hand. But where was Dad?

Zoey heard footsteps coming downstairs.

At last!

But it wasn't Dad. It was Marcus. "Wow, where are *you* going?" she asked him. "Got a big date?" He was wearing a shirt with an actual collar and a jacket over that.

He grinned. "What do you mean, where am I going? I thought there was a big fashion show tonight and my little sister was the star designer!"

"And you're coming? Marcus? Really?" She'd never even thought to ask him if he would.

"Well, sure." Marcus shrugged. "Why wouldn't I?" he asked.

Oh, for a million reasons, thought Zoey, starting with the fact that the idea of watching a bunch of middle school girls parade around in borrowed dresses had to be the last thing he would want to do on a Friday night.

"I mean, if you don't want me to come," he started. "If I'll embarrass you or something, I totally get it."

"No . . . *come!* I want you to."

Ding-dong.

Zoey spun around, surprised again, this time by someone at the door. She pulled it open. "Aunt Lulu! Whoa! It's really raining outside, huh!"

Her aunt nodded as she shook out her umbrella and stepped in from the front porch. "Pouring!" She leaned over to give Zoey a peck on each of her cheeks. "Ooh! Is this it?" She stepped up to Zoey's dress and traced one of the buttons. "I love it!" She smiled at Zoey. "And you look pretty fabulous yourself. You too, Marcus!"

Zoey grinned. "Thanks, Aunt Lulu."

"Thanks!" said Marcus, with a twinkle in his eye. "I was going for fabulous."

Zoey playfully stuck her tongue out at him.

Finally, her dad appeared on the landing. "Sorry I'm late. The father of the designer has to look sharp!" He was wearing Zoey's *least*—not most— favorite tie. It was the one with big yellow ovals that looked like either pineapples . . . or radioactive grenades. She smiled up at him and made a mental note to make him a cool tie. "Oh good, Lulu, you're here!" he continued. "What are we waiting for? Let's go!"

Zoey shared Aunt Lulu's umbrella from the car to the school lobby, but then she said good-bye. "I'll see you guys after the show," she told her family, eager to find her friends backstage.

She ran a few steps down the hall, then paused and turned around.

"Thank you guys so much for coming," she said, dashing to give them each a quick hug.

"Break a leg," said Marcus.

"Isn't that more for *actors*?" Aunt Lulu asked.

Marcus shrugged. "I don't know . . . Break something else then, Zo."

Her dad squeezed her tight. Then did it again. "Your mom would be very proud of you, Zo."

Zoey kissed him and hurried to the backstage entrance, where Libby was waiting.

"Sorry I'm late," Zoey said, panting.

Libby smiled at her. "It's okay. I haven't been here that long. . . ."

"Are you ready?" Zoey asked her.

"Not really." Libby winced.

"You're going to be great!" Zoey told her. "I

can't thank you enough for doing this!"

"I just hope I don't trip or anything. . . ."

"Don't be silly! But if you get nervous, just look for Kate in the crowd. She told me she'll be cheering you on!" Zoey replied. "Shall we go in?" She nodded toward the door.

Libby took a deep breath and nodded. "I guess so," she said taking Zoey's dress bag.

Backstage, a dozen girls were getting ready.

"Yay! There you are!" someone called from across the room.

Zoey turned to see who it was. A pretty girl in an indigo dress was waving. Zoey didn't recognize her until she flashed a smile full of braces.

"*Priti!*" Zoey gasped. "Wow! You look amazing!" Priti ran up and gave her a hug.

"I know! Isn't it great!" she said, spinning around to show off her dress. "I told my mom she has to bid on it or I'll never talk to her again."

"Yeah? And what did she say?" joked Zoey.

Priti rolled her eyes. "She laughed and said she would." She leaned in. "Have you seen Ivy yet?"

"No, we just got here . . . why?" said Zoey.

Priti grinned. "Oh, just wait."

As it turned out, though, they didn't have to.

Priti bit her lip. "Ooh. Here she comes."

Zoey turned and so did Libby, to see Ivy teetering up between Shannon and Bree. Her face was hidden behind thick layers of makeup.

"She looks like she should be in a *pageant*," murmured Libby.

"I know," replied Zoey under her breath. "And look at those shoes. Four-inch platform heels? How's she going to walk in those, do you think, without holding on to Shannon and Bree?"

Ivy didn't seem worried about that. Though she seemed surprised when she noticed Zoey. Her mouth fell open . . . then she turned around.

"I'd walk away too if I were her," said Priti.

Zoey didn't really blame Ivy, though. She didn't think Ivy could be *that* mean, to ruin the dress on purpose. But she also couldn't figure out how the paint fell by mistake or how the garment bag became unzipped. Maybe she would never know what really happened, but she was just relieved that everything had worked out.

"Fifteen minutes!" Zoey heard someone holler.

"Oh my gosh, Zoey!" Libby grabbed her arm. "We should hurry. I have to get dressed!"

Zoey nodded and unzipped the garment bag. "Here!" she said with a satisfied sigh. She pulled out the dress and handed it to Libby.

"Ooh! It's too cute!" she and Priti both squealed. "It looks a lot like the first one."

But as soon as Libby held it up to her body, their voices faded away.

"Um . . ." Libby's face was a collage of a bunch of emotions—none of them very good.

Zoey's stomach, meanwhile, was about to evict the few bites of pizza she'd managed to swallow at home.

"Is it meant to be that short?" asked Priti.

"No," Zoey said. "Not at all."

She'd meant to make it just like she'd made the cover-ups for her and Kate and Priti—one size fits all. But she'd completely forgotten that five-foot-nine Libby was not a one-size-fits-all girl.

"I don't know if I can wear this," said Libby miserably, as if *she'd* done something wrong. "I mean, not without shorts . . . or something . . . you know?"

Zoey nodded. "No. Of course! It's all my fault. I'm sorry, Libby. What a stupid, stupid mistake."

That's what happened when you tried to sew a dress—and write a social studies paper—in just a few days.

Suddenly someone tapped Zoey on the shoulder. She turned. It was Mrs. Diaz, the assistant principal.

"Zoey," she said, "have you seen Ms. Austen? She's been looking all over for you!"

"Really? No." Zoey looked around. *The principal!* she thought. The knot in her stomach wound its way to her throat. The idea of facing Ms. Austen and confessing her latest disaster was almost too much to bear. She turned toward the exit—her closest escape route—and then she heard her name.

"Zoey! There you are!"

She turned to see Ms. Austen walking up in her black dress from that morning, to which she'd added a long rope of pearls. She'd put her hair back in a slick ponytail and swapped strappy red heels for her black patent pumps. In her hands she held a clipboard and a long garment bag. It was all Zoey could do to say "Hi . . ." back. And not burst into tears.

"I am so glad to find you," said Ms. Austen. "I should have called you, I know. But the day got away from me, and well . . ." She sighed. "I knew I'd eventually catch you here. Anyway." She held out the garment bag to Zoey. "This came via overnight delivery today, after school—with your name on it. We're all wondering what's inside."

Her name on it?

"There's a note," said Ms. Austen. She motioned to a square white envelope taped to the front.

Zoey plucked it off and lifted the tab and pulled out a creamy white card. It took her two tries to read the bold, black handwriting on the card.

Dear Sew Zoey,

Keep up the good work!

Best of luck,

Fashionsista

"What does it say?" asked Priti.

Every face around her, including Ms. Austen's, seemed to be asking the same question.

"It's . . . it's from one of my blog followers," said Zoey slowly.

"Well, open it!" Priti said.

Right . . . Zoey took the garment bag from Ms. Austen and slid the zipper down. The sides fell open to reveal a startlingly familiar-looking dress.

"*No. Way.*" Zoey's lips formed the words without making a sound. It was an exact copy of her first dress—right down to the braided cord! The only difference was that this dress was clean and new . . . and made of the kind of luxurious fabric that Zoey drooled over at A Stitch in Time but couldn't actually buy.

There was one other tiny difference also, which Priti was the first to point out.

"Look, Zoey! There's a tag inside!" she said.

Sure enough, there was.

Libby read it for her. "It says 'Sew Zoey.' So cool!"

"I'm confused," said Ms. Austen. "Is this the dress that was ruined? Was it cleaned?"

Zoey looked up at her and shook her head. "No. That dress is at home. . . ." What was left of it, at least. She'd actually torn the seams out and recut the pieces already to make a shoulder bag when she had more time. So . . . unless the dress changed fabrics and had its own time machine, this was definitely not the same one. "I think . . . I don't know how . . . ," Zoey went on, as much to herself as anyone else. "But I think someone made this for me."

"You know what this means!" exclaimed Priti, reaching out to give Zoey a squeeze. "You don't have to worry about that other dress now, Zoey. Libby can wear this one instead!"

"I'll put it on right now!" said Libby. She reached for the hanger. But Zoey held on, looking unsure.

She looked up at Ms. Austen again. "Is that okay?" she slowly asked. "I mean, like I said, this isn't actually the dress I *made*. . . . The only thing is, the second dress I brought in . . . well . . . you can see for yourself . . ." She nodded to the dress still in Libby's hand, and Libby held it up.

"Ooh . . . yes . . . I see. . . ." Ms. Austen frowned,

duly noting where it stopped. "Well, then, I guess you don't have much choice. This is your design, right?" she asked Zoey.

Zoey smiled. "Oh definitely."

"Well, not every designer sews every dress he or she makes," said Ms. Austen. "Why should you live by different rules? Oh, look at that!" She checked her watch, then took a deep breath and smoothed her hair. "It's almost showtime girls. I'd better get back out front. Have fun now!"

The next hour was a blur for Zoey—but this is what she knew for sure: The new dress fit Libby perfectly. Like a gold-trimmed, crimson-red glove.

"How do I look?" Libby asked.

"So great! So awesome!" Zoey said.

"You just need one thing." Priti held up her finger. "Wait here. I'll be right back."

She reappeared in a second with a tube of lip gloss. "There!" She dabbed some on Libby and grinned. "*Now* you're ready to go out there. . . . Oh! Am *I* up already? See you in a little while!"

Libby walked onto the stage a few minutes

later—and Zoey wasn't sure who was more nervous, Libby or her. But by the time she walked off to a round of applause, whoops, and cheers, they were both ready to do it again!

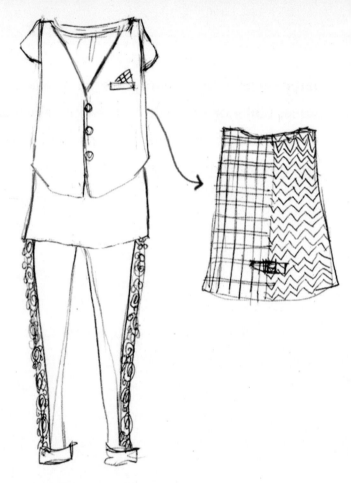

CHAPTER 12

Oh my gosh! Oh my gosh! Oh my gosh!

I don't even know where to begin this post, aside from showing you a sketch of what I wore to the fashion show. Do I tell you all about how amazing the show was and fill you in on the deets? Or do I start off by saying, "Thank you, Fashionsista!" You're my fashion fairy godmother! Honestly! Clearly I have to start with the latter, so here goes: Thank you! Thank you! Thank you! Again and again and again! And for those of you who are wondering, "What for?" I got the most amazing surprise today—and just in the nick of time. The dress I made out of a one-size-fits-all pattern was too short for Libby, and before I had a chance to freak out, I received an exact replica of my original dress in the mail. And, honestly, it looked a million bazillion times better than mine! (That's probably why there was a bidding war and it got the highest bid of the whole night. And who was the big spender? None other than yours truly's dear old dad!) I almost can't believe the whole thing is over now—and here's the craziest thing: Now that it is, I'm already holding my breath, waiting to do it again! Okay, I know, I'm crazy. But I never said that I wasn't, now, did I? Uh-oh! Speaking of waiting, I've got to go. My friends are calling (hollering, actually). TTFN Zo

PS To anyone who's dying to solve the Case of the Destroyed Dress, I've decided to let it go. I mean, even if someone ruined it, which I'm not saying they did, everything worked out fine in the end. But thanks for being in my corner! You're the bestest web friends ever.

"There. I just had to post that," said Zoey, returning to Priti, Libby, and Kate. "Hey! Did you guys already eat all that popcorn? Thanks a lot!" she teased, eyeing the few kernels left in the bowl.

"Oops! Sorry," said Libby.

"Well, you know what they say: You snooze, you lose,'" Priti joked. "Or 'you blog, you lose'?"

"I guess we'll just have to make some more," said Kate cheerfully.

They were all gathered in Zoey's bedroom, where they'd come straight from the fashion show for a slumber party. Zoey had begged her dad to let them sleep over, and there'd been no way he could say no. Zoey, of course, had to go online right away and post a quick update on her blog. She wanted especially for Fashionsista to read it and know how happy and grateful she was for her amazing gift. But now she was done and 100 percent ready to celebrate with her friends.

"Good idea!" she told Kate. She opened her door. "Come on. Let's go downstairs. I don't know why—maybe it's because I was too nervous to eat dinner—but I'm really *starving!*" Zoey said.

They loped down to the kitchen, passing the family room where Zoey's dad and Marcus were watching TV.

"Everything okay, girls?" her dad called out.

"Everything's great, Dad!" Zoey told him.

In the kitchen, she found the popcorn and slipped a bag in the microwave while her friends plopped down on stools. There were four vases on the counter in front of them, each holding a big bouquet. The dahlias were from Aunt Lulu—from her garden, in fact. The gerbera daisies were from Dad and Marcus, and the tiger lilies were a surprise from Jan. The fourth bouquet, the roses, came with thanks from the Mapleton music department and was the same sunny orange as the ones on the desk in Ms. Austen's office.

"*Mmm.*" Kate leaned in to smell each one, then suddenly she laughed.

"What?" Zoey asked.

"Oh, I was just remembering Ivy. . . . It's not really that funny, but she did look silly when she tripped onstage!"

"Oh my gosh! I heard the whole auditorium gasp. What happened?" Priti asked.

Kate threw up her hands. "Who knows? One minute she's limping across the stage in those platforms—and the next minute she's stumbling toward the edge. She's fine, though!" Kate said.

"*That* is what's known as *karma*!" Priti said with a satisfied nod.

Beep-beep-beep!

The air in the kitchen thickened with buttery smells as the microwave timer went off.

Zoey popped open the door and grabbed the bag and tossed it in front of the other girls.

Priti picked it up, then promptly dropped it. "Ooh! That's hot!" she gasped.

"Here, let me," said Kate, taking the bag with two fingers and expertly prying it open. A salty cloud of steam burst out, and she leaned away as she dumped the bag into the bowl. "Yum!" She helped herself to a handful after blowing on it first. Then she paused, and her face began twisting as she tried to suck out a kernel wedged in one of the brackets. "I'll be so glad when these braces are *off* and eating popcorn won't be such an ordeal," she said and groaned.

Libby reached for a kernel. "You know . . . ," she said, "speaking of ordeals, I bet Ivy was still thinking about Zoey's dress when she tripped. Kate, you should have seen her when Zoey took out the dress. I thought her makeup was going to melt off her face, she looked so upset!"

"And *you* didn't see her when *you* put it on," said Zoey. "You looked amazing, Libby."

Libby blushed. "It was all the dress," she said, waving the compliment away.

"Ah-hem." Priti cleared her throat.

"And you looked great too, of course!" Zoey laughed.

"Thank you." Priti nodded. "It was *mostly* the dress," she joked. "But, seriously, Zoey, don't you want to know what happened?"

"Well, I really thought it was probably just bad luck and that no one was to blame," Zoey said. "But that look on Ivy's face said it all. After the show, I told her we needed to talk. She admitted it was her fault. . . ."

Priti, Libby, and Kate all gasped.

"But she also said it was a mistake, and I believe her," Zoey said. Her friends sat there, entranced, eating popcorn mindlessly, as if they were watching a movie instead of listening to Zoey explain what happened. "She said she snuck into the room to get a peek at the dress. She was rushing to put it back in the garment bag and knocked over the can of paint. She didn't know what to do, and she was too embarrassed to tell anyone."

"I can't believe it!" said Libby.

"Wow . . . ," said Priti, after a rare moment of speechlessness.

Just then the phone rang. Zoey picked it up and heard a familiar voice. It was Ms. Austen. She put her finger in front of her mouth to hush her friends.

"Hello? Zoey?"

"Y-yes, hi, Ms. Austen," Zoey stammered.

"Zoey, I'm sorry to bother you at home, but I just read your blog post, and, well, I had to talk with you about those last few lines. Did someone ruin your dress? If so, that's not something I would want to let slide."

"Oh. Well, not exactly," Zoey said. "Besides, it all worked out, anyway."

"Are you sure, Zoey?" Ms. Austen asked.

"Yes," Zoey replied. "I'm sure."

"If you change your mind, we can talk about it," Ms. Austen said.

"Thanks, Ms. Austen." Zoey hung up the phone.

Her friends were even more shocked than she was.

Libby was the first to speak. "That was your big chance to give Ivy what she deserved!"

"But it wasn't on purpose," Zoey said. "She was just too scared to tell anyone about it. And I think tripping onstage was bad enough."

Libby nodded in agreement. It was the exact thing she'd said she was scared of doing on the runway.

"See? Pure *karma*!" said Priti as she walked over to the fridge to get a drink. "Anyway, let's talk about something more fun. Who is this *Fashionsista*? That's I want to know!"

"Yeah, we have to find out!" Kate said. "Hey, Priti, is that a Coke? Can I have one?"

Priti slid three cans across the island, one for each of her friends. "Do you think it's that fabric store lady?" she said. "Hey, I bet it is! Don't you?"

Zoey shrugged. *Jan?* "Huh . . . maybe," she said. She knew Jan read her blog now . . . so it was possible.

"I bet Tara could find out," said Priti. "She knows all that computer stuff. Want me to ask her?" she asked Zoey.

"I don't know . . . ," Zoey said. She helped herself to some popcorn and flipped the tab on her drink. "No . . . that's okay," she finally said.

It was kind of fun having a mysterious fairy godmother out there. And it was even more fun that she saved the day at Zoey's first fashion show. But the most fun thing of all? That this was just the beginning . . . and the future was looking *sew* good.

Want to know *sew* much more?

Here's a sneak peek at the next book in the Sew Zoey series:

on PINS AND NEEDLES

Plenty of Pom-Poms!

Three guesses where I'm going today—and the first two don't count. The Eastern State University football game, you say? Congratulations! You are right! And, no, I am not wearing a "pom-pom dress." It's what I wish the ESU cheerleaders could be wearing instead of the same old uniforms they've been sporting ever since I've been going to their games. And that's . . . let's see . . . If I'm twelve years old . . . that means twelve years, approximately.

That probably sounds like I'm a huge, crazy football fan, doesn't it? But I'm not really, so let me explain. If my dad didn't work at ESU as a physical therapist for all the sports teams, trust me, I'd be at home sewing and sketching (and blogging!) on Saturdays instead of watching a football game—or basketball or baseball . . . You name it and we're there. It's not so bad, though, when my friends Kate and Priti come with, which they are today. Hooray!

If you'll be there, look for us. I'll be the one with the sketchbook—because you never know when inspiration will hit! Oh, and I'll be wearing the top that I finally finished, which I blogged about yesterday. Some might think it's a little fancy for a football game, but I think it's just too cute not to wear right away. Too bad I didn't make it Eagles colors—purple and yellow. Hmm. Those colors look pretty good together. Something to think about . . . !

TTFN. Go, Eagles!

(Did I really just say that?! OMG! I better go sew something, so I feel like myself again.)

"Here it comes!" said Priti Holbrooke. She pointed to the end of the football field.

"I see it." Zoey Webber leaned forward and perched on the edge of the hard metal seat.

On her other side was Kate Mackey, whose big blue eyes were focused on the game. Zoey nudged her. "It's coming. Get ready," she said.

"What?" Kate turned to look. She groaned, but she was smiling as she leaned forward as well.

A second later, the wave reached them. They stood and threw their arms into the air: Kate's long tan ones; Zoey's pale, freckled ones; and Priti's, which were cinnamon brown.

"Whooo!" Zoey yelled—not quite as loud as Priti, but close—then they all sat back down and watched the wave continue around.

"That's fifteen!" Priti exclaimed. "How high do you think it'll go?"

Kate glanced at the clock. "Well, it's almost half-time, so it'll have to stop pretty soon."

Suddenly the crowd jumped back up and an even louder cry rang out. Zoey looked down to see the whole ESU team celebrating what must have been an exciting touchdown.

"Oh! I missed it!" cried Kate. She shook her head in disbelief.

Zoey rubbed her shoulder. "Sorry," she said. Kate took sports very seriously, and since Zoey took fashion very seriously, she knew how she must feel. Not as bad, of course, as Zoey had felt when the dress she'd designed and sewn for their school's fashion show was mysteriously ruined by yellow paint. More like when she realized she'd mixed up the sleeves on the top she was wearing that day. She'd almost cried when she had to rip them out and start all over again. In the end, though, it turned out fine. Better than she'd hoped. The top was supersimple . . . looking. Basically, a loose-fitting tee. The fabric, though, was a fabulous blue and green ikat for the bodice, and a magenta and gold one for the sleeves.

"Don't worry, they'll do it again," she told Kate.

"Let's hope so," Kate said as she looked at the scoreboard, which was: VISITORS 21, ESU EAGLES 6.

Priti leaned over Zoey to give Kate a pat on the knee. "Hey, guys. Spirit!" she said. "That's what wins games. Hey! You want some stickers to put on your cheeks?" She pointed to her own, on which tiny gold eagles were perched, and flashed her signature wide Holbrooke grin. "Oh, look out, look out!" she said suddenly. "Here comes another wave!"

By halftime the wave count was twenty. The score hadn't changed. And Zoey was getting hungry. It seemed like way more than two hours since she'd had lunch at home with her dad.

"Snack bar?" she asked her friends, who each instantly jumped up.

"You read my mind! I'm absolutely starving," said Kate, already scooting toward the aisle.

Zoey stopped in front of her dad, who'd been sitting behind them with friends from work. They were all wearing ESU caps, which were purple with gold letters across the front. Only her dad had on The Tie, though, which he always wore for good luck. It was bright purple with gold winking eagles and frankly made Zoey's eyes hurt.

Zoey loved her dad more than anything . . . but he was style challenged, to say the least. She sometimes wondered if her mom was alive, would he have still worn the things he did? Zoey was too young when her mom died to remember her well, but everyone still talked about her style and how chic she always looked.

In fact, Zoey wondered a lot of things about what having her mom would be like.

"Hey, Dad? Okay if we go get some popcorn?" she called to him.

He nodded. "Sure. Bring some back for me?"

Zoey held out her hand and opened and closed it, the international sign for "Money, please."

"Thank you!" she said as he handed her a bill.

"Yeah, thanks!" Priti and Kate chimed in.

Together, they hurried down the bleacher steps to the nearest snack bar. The air smelled of salty popcorn and greasy hot dogs, and the line was already long. Zoey read the menu to see what else they might want. . . .

"Ooh, look!" she said. "They have gummy bears!"

Kate made a face, and so did Priti, and Zoey quickly remembered why. Both of her friends had braces, which made gummy bears—and a million other things—almost impossible to eat. Kate had been the first one to get them, and Zoey still remembered how jealous she'd been. "Why can't I get braces?" she'd asked her dad again and again.

"Because you don't need them," he'd told her proudly. "You have straight teeth—like your mom." Personally, Zoey would rather have gotten her mom's strawberry-blonde hair instead of the wavy brown stuff she got from her dad. But she also knew now that braces weren't half as much fun as she'd thought they were when she was ten.

"Popcorn's bad enough," said Priti. "I still have some stuck in my mouth from last week."

"I know." Kate nodded. "I'm going to be so happy on Monday. I can't wait!"

"Monday?" Priti flashed a sneaky look at Zoey. "Why?" she asked. "What happens then?"

Kate's mouth fell open, stunned. "I'm getting my braces off. How could you forget?"

"Oh, right." Priti nodded this time. "Of course. Silly me." She started to smile at Zoey, but Zoey had to look away. She knew if her eyes met Priti's right then, she could easily blow their "bye-bye braces" surprise for Kate. . . .